THE
JOURNEY
PRIZE

STORIES

WINNERS OF THE $10,000 JOURNEY PRIZE

1989: Holley Rubinsky for "Rapid Transits"

1990: Cynthia Flood for "My Father Took a Cake to France"

1991: Yann Martel for "The Facts Behind the Helsinki Roccamatios"

1992: Rozena Maart for "No Rosa, No District Six"

1993: Gayla Reid for "Sister Doyle's Men"

1994: Melissa Hardy for "Long Man the River"

1995: Kathryn Woodward for "Of Marranos and Gilded Angels"

1996: Elyse Gasco for "Can You Wave Bye Bye, Baby?"

1997 (shared): Gabriella Goliger for "Maladies of the Inner Ear"
                     Anne Simpson for "Dreaming Snow"

1998: John Brooke for "The Finer Points of Apples"

1999: Alissa York for "The Back of the Bear's Mouth"

2000: Timothy Taylor for "Doves of Townsend"

2001: Kevin Armstrong for "The Cane Field"

2002: Jocelyn Brown for "Miss Canada"

2003: Jessica Grant for "My Husband's Jump"

2004: Devin Krukoff for "The Last Spark"

2005: Matt Shaw for "Matchbook for a Mother's Hair"

2006: Heather Birrell for "BriannaSusannaAlana"

2007: Craig Boyko for "OZY"

2008: Saleema Nawaz for "My Three Girls"

2009: Yasuko Thanh for "Floating Like the Dead"

2010: Devon Code for "Uncle Oscar"

2011: Miranda Hill for "Petitions to Saint Chronic"

2012: Alex Pugsley for "Crisis on Earth-X"

2013: Naben Ruthnum for "Cinema Rex"

2014: Tyler Keevil for "Sealskin"

2015: Deirdre Dore for "The Wise Baby"

The BEST of CANADA'S NEW WRITERS

THE
JOURNEY
PRIZE

STORIES

SELECTED BY

KATE CAYLEY
BRIAN FRANCIS
MADELEINE THIEN

McCLELLAND & STEWART

Library and Archives of Canada Cataloguing in Publication is available upon request

Published simultaneously in the United States of America by McClelland & Stewart, a division of Penguin Random House Canada Limited

Library of Congress Control Number available upon request

ISBN: 978-0-7710-5086-2
ebook ISBN: 978-0-7710-5087-9

The quotation on p. 107 is taken from the academic paper "Past, present & future scenario of thalassaemic care & control in India" by Ishwar C. Verma, Renu Saxena, and Sudha Kohli, published in *Indian Journal of Medical Research* (October 2011; 134(4): 507–521).

The quotation in the last line of p.111 is from *The Origin of Species* by Charles Darwin.

Typeset in Janson by M&S, Toronto
Cover design: Leah Springate

Printed and bound in the United States of America

McClelland & Stewart,
a division of Penguin Random House Canada Limited,
a Penguin Random House Company
www.penguinrandomhouse.ca

1   2   3   4   5   20   19   18   17   16

 Penguin
Random
House

ABOUT THE JOURNEY PRIZE STORIES

The $10,000 Journey Prize is awarded annually to an emerging writer of distinction. This award, now in its twenty-eighth year, and given for the sixteenth time in association with the Writers' Trust of Canada as the Writers' Trust of Canada/ McClelland & Stewart Journey Prize, is made possible by James A. Michener's generous donation of his Canadian royalty earnings from his novel *Journey*, published by McClelland & Stewart in 1988. The Journey Prize itself is the most significant monetary award given in Canada to a developing writer for a short story or excerpt from a fiction work in progress. The winner of this year's Journey Prize will be selected from among the eleven stories in this book.

The Journey Prize Stories has established itself as the most prestigious annual fiction anthology in the country, introducing readers to the finest new literary writers from coast to coast for more than two decades. It has become a who's who of up-and-coming writers, and many of the authors who have appeared in the anthology's pages have gone on to distinguish themselves with short story collections, novels, and literary awards. The anthology comprises a selection from submissions made by the editors of literary journals from across the country, who have chosen what, in their view, is the most exciting writing in English that they have published in the previous year. In recognition of the vital role journals play in fostering literary voices, McClelland & Stewart makes its own award of $2,000 to the journal that originally published and submitted the winning entry.

This year the selection jury comprised three acclaimed writers:

Kate Cayley's first collection of short fiction, *How You Were Born*, won the 2015 Trillium Book Award and was a finalist for the Governor General's Award. She has also published a collection of poetry, *When This World Comes to an End*. She is currently a playwright-in-residence at Tarragon Theatre, and has written two plays for Tarragon, *After Akhmatova* and *The Bakelite Masterpiece*. Her second collection of poetry, *Other Houses*, is forthcoming from Brick Books. She lives in Toronto.

Brian Francis is the author of two novels. His most recent, *Natural Order*, was selected by the *Toronto Star*, Kobo, and *Georgia Straight* as a Best Book of 2011. His first novel, *Fruit*, was a 2009 Canada Reads finalist and was selected as a Barnes and Noble Discover Great New Writers title. He lives in Toronto.

Madeleine Thien is the author of the story collection *Simple Recipes*, and the novels *Certainty* and *Dogs at the Perimeter*, which was shortlisted for Berlin's 2014 International Literature Award and won the Frankfurt Book Fair's 2015 Liberaturpreis. Her books and stories have been translated into twenty-five languages. Her essays have appeared in *Granta*, the *Guardian*, the *Financial Times*, *Five Dials*, *Brick*, and elsewhere, and her story "The Wedding Cake" was shortlisted for the 2015 *Sunday Times* EFG Short Story Award. A new novel, *Do Not Say We Have Nothing*, will be published in 2016. She lives in Montreal.

The jury read a total of eighty-seven submissions without knowing the names of the authors or those of the journals in which the stories originally appeared. McClelland & Stewart would like to thank the jury for their efforts in selecting this year's anthology and, ultimately, the winner of this year's Journey Prize.

McClelland & Stewart would also like to acknowledge the continuing enthusiastic support of writers, literary journal editors, and the public in the common celebration of new voices in Canadian fiction.

For more information about *The Journey Prize Stories*, please visit www.facebook.com/TheJourneyPrize.

CONTENTS

READING THE 2016 JOURNEY PRIZE STORIES

BRIAN FRANCIS

I remember hearing once that a short story should be short enough to read in one sitting. (Or one standing, if you're on the subway, which is where I do most of my reading.) I get the sentiment as far as length, but what are the general rules when it comes to short stories? What makes a short story good? What makes it exceptional? What makes you miss your subway stop?

I can't speak for my fellow jurors, but I was hesitant when I was asked to be a Journey Prize juror. As a writer, I'm not entirely comfortable judging the work of other writers. I know what goes into writing. The energy. The emotion. The time. But as I worked my way through these stories, and when Madeleine, Kate, and I met to discuss them, I realized that it wasn't so much about judging other people's work as it was about honouring excellence.

Ultimately, the stories in this collection are here because they're spectacular in their own ways, bright constellations of imagination, conflict, and depth. But they're also here because of the choices each writer made. Writing, after all, is a playground of choice: choices of words, of scenes, of characters, of tone, of subject matter. All of these writers have made very wise choices. Most of all, they invite you, the reader, into their work. The door is open. Step in. Wander around. Immerse yourself in the talents of eleven exceptional writers and their stories.

Keep an eye out for your subway stop.

KATE CAYLEY

A woman obsessively visits the gym after breaking up with her girlfriend. A veteran of the war in Afghanistan finds himself shooting a bear in the ballroom of an upscale hotel. A woman who works in a plant that processes chickens warily observes her co-workers' desperate attempts at escape. A miner may or may not be pursued by the devil in the dark. Missives are sent from Mars to an unresponsive Earth, as hundreds of years earlier, a man writes letters to a homeland he will never see again. As this year's jury carefully, and sometimes with difficulty, selected the stories for this anthology, I felt blessed and invigorated by the sheer variety of voices we encountered and was reminded of the John Berger quotation, "Never again will a single story be told as though it were the only one." These were stories told in many styles, from delicate to brash to deeply strange, in voices that were sometimes baroque and sometimes heartbreakingly simple. I was buoyed up by the quality of each one, but even more by how wide-ranging the collection was as a whole.

In selecting the stories for the Journey Prize anthology, we found some patterns emerged. Some writers were far along in their craft, others less so. Interestingly, the experiences of clever people in cities or hoping to be in cities seems to be replacing stories of life in small towns as the cliché of choice. Some stories toppled under the weight of their conceptual frameworks. Others didn't have enough meat on the bones. Others showed promise in the evidence of a brilliant eye, but were too profuse in their details. But in the end, we had to set aside many good stories, stories that were beautiful, funny, sharp, and full of feeling, stories that, just as much as the ones in this collection, represented a wide range of both style and experience. To the writers in this collection: thank you. To the writers who very nearly were, whose stories we set aside with regret and admiration: thank you also.

MADELEINE THIEN

A description of the gym in Alex Leslie's "The Person You Want to See" describes perfectly, for me, the experience of reading these stories—descending into the "aquarium intimacy" of overlapping private worlds. One moment we're a male manicurist, then we're abandoned on a planetary outpost, or we're hip deep in a river as salmon blaze past to their end. The tensions between these stories are visceral and moving and sometimes disturbing.

Together they reveal a network of defended privacies and unusual hauntings: ghosts, refugees, forgotten wars, hunted animals, deleted Facebook posts, embryos, genes, history, and even the memory of salvation. The stories describe our contemporary world, but they confront us with our own alienness, all the things we never noticed or thought worthy of noticing. How do they do this? By committing entirely—word and sentence, feeling and intellect—to their imagined realities. When someone believes in something, it makes me pay attention. My antennae lift. There's energy here, between me and the writer, a necessary, though often challenging, friction.

Leslie quotes a trainer's advice, "The ultimate test of strength is to be able to hold up your own weight. Hold yourself aloft." This is a mesmerizing way to think about each story. Can it hold up its own weight? Does it attempt to carry too much, and in so doing, manage to hoist—briefly, impossibly—another weight entirely? The reader, too, becomes another person inside that brevity, "close to it and out of sight," as Souvankham Thammavongsa memorably observes in "Mani Pedi." What I love about these stories is that each, in its own perilous way, chooses the uneasy path. My heartfelt admiration to the writers. I wish them all the best with the literature yet to come.

SOUVANKHAM THAMMAVONGSA

PARIS

The sky was black like the middle of an eye. Red revved the engine, impatient, having to wait for the truck to warm up. It was an old thing. A thing she saw on someone's front lawn. The make was nothing special. They call it a pickup truck, but she never picked anything up in it. Just herself. It might have been the colour that drew Red to it. And the thing was big. It took up most of the lane on the road. It might have been the thought of that big red thing in the parking lot at the plant. It would be the best-looking thing. And it was hers. She wanted that. Especially.

Red worked at the plant like most of the others in town. It was her job to pluck the feathers, make sure the chickens were smooth when they left her. By the time the chickens got to her they were already dead. Their eyes closed tight like they were sleeping. It was almost like what happened in the other room didn't happen at all. Sometimes she could swear she heard the chickens in the other room—that sudden desperate flap of wing, as if flight could really take place there.

Red looked at her face in the rear-view mirror. It didn't show her whole face, just the eyes. She lifted herself from the driver's seat, turned her head to the right side, looked at her profile, and imagined what she would look like with a different nose. How maybe if she looked different, things would be different at the plant. Especially with Tommy. Tommy was her boss, her supervisor, married with two young boys. He was nice to her. Gave her more shifts than anyone else and complimented her work.

"You did good, Red. Keep it up. We've got plans for you." What those plans were, she never knew. Just that they had them for her. Sometimes Tommy would buy her a cola from the machine or sit at her table during her lunch breaks. They talked mostly about his boys and how he was planning a trip to Paris with his wife for Valentine's Day. His wife, Nicole, had a nose Red wished she could have. It was a thin nose that stuck out from her face and pointed upward. Anyone who worked in the front office had that kind of nose. His wife always came to the plant's annual Christmas party, wearing something fashionable, with fabric no one else's clothes were made out of. The fabric was thick and fit her tightly, smoothed out and pressed, not a wrinkle in sight. At the party, she stood the whole time in a group with the other wives whose husbands ran or owned the company. They would all come say hello to each person who worked there, introduce themselves, and then go stand huddled in a corner with each other, like they did some great charity work, conversing.

Every year, at the party, it was fried chicken. It never bothered Red that the pieces she ate could have been one of those dead chickens that came to her to get plucked. Cut up into pieces like that, there wasn't a face to think of. And every year, she looked forward to this party, wore her best clothes to it: a pair of jeans, a blue-and-white checkered shirt, and thick black boots from Canadian Tire. It wasn't fancy like the other girls, and it didn't show much, but there wasn't much Red wanted to show. It had become a trend a few years ago when one of the girls who worked there got a nose job. Her glasses didn't have to be held up with an elastic band at the back of the head. The girl got her hair done after that, every week. She already had a small thin body. Cute, was what Tommy called it. Then, she started getting more shifts and eventually got a job at the front office. The front office! It was hard to believe someone like them could get a job there. In this town, a girl either worked at the chicken plant or the Boobie Bungalow. At least at the Boobie Bungalow, you could make some quick cash and get the hell out of town, never look back, or you could get someone who could love you just long enough to take you out of the town. A man you met there was single or on his way to being single. At the plant, most of the men were married and if they weren't they would be eventually, to someone else who didn't work at the plant. You made enough money to pay for what you needed, but the big things in life, the things that could make you happy, well, you just never made enough to get those. Red knew, for her, it was going to be the chicken plant. She didn't have much in the chest area, and couldn't dance to music even if it had a beat. The way men never looked at her gave her the sense the Boobie Bungalow just wasn't for her.

The girl who worked in the front office stood, at the Christmas party, with Tommy's wife and the other wives as if she was now one of them. They didn't talk to her or include her in their conversations, but she was happy she could stand there with them, and not with Red and the others on the line. All of their noses looked the same, sticking out in the air like that. But now, the girl doesn't work at the plant anymore. Something about Nicole and the other wives not liking her there. They thought the girl didn't belong in the front office with their husbands but at the back, on the line, plucking feathers like Red. The girl was asked to take her job on the line again. She quit after that, on account of having been someplace better.

After the front office job became available again, all the women wanted the job. The girls out back started to get nose jobs. Where they found a surgeon was something Red didn't know. No facility around here to support that kind of thing. Maybe that's why everyone's nose didn't quite look the same; some were slightly bent, didn't heal properly, or scarred badly. One girl, when she talked, her nose moved in every direction that her upper lip moved. It was like her nose was attached to that lip. Most of the girls at the plant started to come dressed in heels and fancy clothes, their hair curled and pressed. They'd change into their work gear, the plastic shower cap and the matching white plastic pullover. They would change right back when their shift was over. They all seemed so glamorous.

"Hey, Dang!" Somboun said. Dang was what people who knew Red called her. It means red in Lao. It wasn't her real name, a nickname she got because her nose was always red from the cold. She hated that he called her by a nickname. It made things feel intimate in a way she didn't want.

"I didn't get one!" she said, referring to the nose job.

"You look fine the way you are." He knew what she was talking about.

"Thanks, Sam." Red knew he hated to be called Sam. He hated his English name and always corrected people, not Sam but Somboun. He was proud in that kind of way.

Red didn't want his attention. Somboun was quiet, kept to himself around others. She rarely saw him during his work hours. He was the one who slit the necks before they got to Red, in another room. He saw the chickens when they were alive. She shuddered at the thought of doing anything with Somboun. What kind of gentleness could a man who did that for a living be capable of?

"Hey, Dang?" Somboun called, trying to keep her attention.

"What is it?" Red said irritably, hoping not to encourage anything further.

"Did you hear about Khet? It was cancer. Started a few months after her nose job. Might have something to do with the material they put in there. Just something to think about."

Red glared at him, annoyed with all his hope.

∞

It was time to break for lunch. It was only twenty minutes. Enough time to use the washroom and gobble down some food. Red saw Tommy come by the line, tap the shoulder of one of the girls who worked for him. She was selected for that day. They walked to his car, where all of it took place.

Just as they were getting into the car, Tommy's wife pulled in the parking lot.

She didn't even bother to park properly.

Nicole wore a white fur coat, her blond curls bounced fresh from the salon. She had bright red lipstick on and rouged cheeks. She was glamorous, beautiful.

She was yelling at him about something. Furious.

Nicole grabbed Tommy by the arm. She didn't fall. She clung to a sleeve, her white heels dragged in the snow. The bottom of her white fur coat was dirty with mud. What she wanted there didn't matter to Tommy. He shut the car door and drove away with the girl in the car. If Red had not come upon this scene, she might have thought the mud was shit. Might have asked how the shit got all over her like that. Women like Nicole are what the romantic movies were made for. They are always the star of their own lives and they always got their man in the end. It's one thing to be ugly, like Red thought she herself was, and to be able to hide in plain sight, to be invisible, and unknown to that kind of advance from Tommy, to have never known that public declaration of love in front of family and friends like Nicole, only to know that simple uncomplicated lonely love one feels for oneself in the quiet moments of the day in the laughter and talk of the television at night and grocery aisles on the weekends. Beauty, for all its ambitions and desires and fuss, seemed so awful to carry and maintain. There's so much to lose. Red felt grateful for what she was to others, ugly.

Nicole spotted Red and trotted over. She grabbed Red and held her like they were the closest of friends. Nicole buried her pointy nose into Red's neck. She could feel the poke. Nicole probably would have done that to anyone standing there. Probably. They stood there together in each other's arms for some time. Both women cried, but for different reasons.

ALEX LESLIE

THE PERSON YOU WANT TO SEE

Bodies open and close on the machines that fill the weight room. A man drags steel from his chest—front push, cheeks taut, and the winged twin paths of his arms move to full extension. His chest under the surgical light. Mechanical bird, his slow flight. Then, release. Arms in, he folds back in, weights clink into a neat stack. He rises, breathes, heads to the water fountain in the corner. At intervals, everyone in the room goes to that fountain, bends down to accept its hook of water into their mouths. The gym is at the front of the community centre, its long glass wall facing the street. The thick rainfall casts the gym in aquarium intimacy. Cars whip past, their headlights the eyebeams of giant fish. Inside, bodies struggle in the tinted air.

Laura watches her body in the floor-to-ceiling mirror. Knee-length black shorts, a black T-shirt, broad shoulders. Behind her, women power the treadmills, knees and elbows in suspended animation. She is always the only woman on the weight machines. Men acknowledge her with nods. She knows them by the slogans on their giveaway T-shirts (*RUN FOR THE CURE 1998 Home Hardware CREW, Who are you RUNNING for*). Nobody speaks to her here and that is part of why she continues to come back.

⤬

In the locker room, women peel clothes from their bodies. Steam is carried out of the showers on their shoulders and hips. A locker door bangs and shatters the warmth. Laughter of the exercise bike women entering in a crowd. After the quiet of the office and her condo, the locker room is jarring for Laura, a thousand electric shocks to her eardrums. As she adjusts her bra, Laura notices the clusters of red specks on her shoulders. She checks the other shoulder. The same. Twists her head to inspect again. A pattern of delicate explosions, where the blood vessels submitted.

That night in bed, laptop nestled on her crossed knees, she Googles: *blood vessels shoulders woman lifting weights.* The fitness pages instruct her to exhale while taking on more weight. Ease the speed of flow. Too much muscle development too fast and the body begins to break itself down, cell by cell. Gradual release of breath is easier on the blood. Trails leave her shoulders, head for her arms. She checks the rest of her body for implosions. Finds none. If she held her breath and lifted hard, how many marks could she make? Her body a map of ruined currents. She twists her torso, holds still for the MacBook camera's inbuilt eye to take a photo of one shoulder. She saves the image to the desktop.

When she double-clicks on the image of her shoulder, it springs up, huge, fills the screen. A planet in low light, a maroon edge, a dark world.

She Googles weightlifters, selects Images. Men with skin-tight balloons defending their necks, shoulders, chests. Their surplus limbs; her faint red trails.

∞∞∞

Laura has been coming to the gym every day for two months and she has felt the change. Not the slimming she expected, but a shift in texture. The ease of heaving the steel and glass doors to the government building where she works, doors that make the sound of a bank vault opening and closing. On mornings after she has lain in bed all night awake, the unexpected panic of being alone coming and going in surges, she climbs the stairs slowly and the secretary at the front desk nods sympathetically, knowingly. Her name is Phillipa and her son's wife passed away five years ago, so she makes a point of over-identifying with every loss in the office—deaths of pets, ailing parents, breakups. Phillipa left a card on Laura's desk when the news about Mallory got around. On the front of the card, a boy reached upward to catch a star, a Little Prince knock-off, a halo of text around his head that read *You don't know what you're reaching for until you find it.* As if someone had died. Also? What an invasive bitch. But maybe Laura's getting bitter. Mostly she's just so tired, all the time. But when she feels her arms they are hard and widening.

Laura's job at the passport office rigidified as routine several years ago. She used to complain about it to Mallory—the endless supply of people who took bureaucracy *personally*, scream at her earnestly over the phone, *but my flight for Cuba is tomorroooooow*—but now, she learns how routine is a crutch for numbness. Routine is everything to her now.

And today, the gift from Phillipa of a meditation book (left anonymously at her desk). Laura picks it up, makes sure to look down at it with a neutral expression—a careful performance for whoever is watching. She leaves the book on the magazine rack in the reception area with the VISA pamphlets after reading the first line on the back: *What you are experiencing is loss.*

Walking to her car, she texts her brother, Greg.

> *Generous anonymous coworker*
> *AKA Philipa Lady of Perpetual*
> *Mourning left book informing me I am having a loss*

His response buzzes her hand as she slips her phone into her pocket. Greg, now thirty-two, texts like an irate teenager.

> *why r anonymous ppl*
> *all such fuckwits do*
> *they have meetings*
>
> *u need a new job*

Then,

> *ROBOOOOOTS!!!!!!*
> *!!!!!!!!!!!!!!!!!!!!!!!!!!*

Yeah.

u could move now
why keep the condo

big

Yes I am considering a year long
cycle tour through the
countryside.
Thank you.

haha fuck you too
☺

Fifteen minutes later, he texts:

what you are experien
cing is losing

loss

sorry

———∞∞∞———

Laura has watched other people go through breakups on Facebook. The suggestive status updates, half-scripts of a melodrama, the sound of a palm clapping on a hard bright screen. Sometimes a few old photos of the couple from early days, posted ambiguously—these photos had a tendency to disappear. It was what people posted and quickly deleted that was most self-revealing, Laura thought. People thought people didn't see, but that's what everybody wanted—the satisfaction of watching life through a two-way mirror. Then, eventually, the Rumi and Hafiz quotes on letting go, the Facebook mourner giving public signs of personal growth. The appropriate I-am-moving-on updates always earned many heart icons (Laura hated these); any persisting bitter or wounded posts were quietly ignored, or condemned by receiving supportive comments only from the mourner's parents. *Things will look up love mom.* Laura has scrolled through many divorces. She read those stories distantly—the grinning avatars amassing sympathy. Facebook was not the place for tough love—you just looked like an asshole. *Have some self-respect*, she'd thought. This too shall pass. It was something buried deep inside her, this reticence. Really, Facebook was only about who was watching you, not what you posted. Still, she couldn't stop scrolling.

When she starts to think about returning to Facebook, Laura isn't surprised to get unsolicited advice from Greg. Over the past three months, he's called her up a few times a week from Halifax, making his two older kids warble pitchy hellos to Laura over the phone. In the summers during his undergrad in public health he'd worked as a tree planter on Vancouver Island. He's always had an effortless builder's body. Laura dreads telling him about her weightlifting—doesn't want to weather his enthusiasm. An outlet, he will say. *I'm so glad you've found an outlet*. Like she's an electrical plug. These days Greg works part-time from home as a graphic designer. In his spare time he makes prints of his photos of trees. He gave Laura and Mallory a triptych of wind-bent arbutus trees for their third anniversary—trunks entwined, sinewy, red and gold. His wife's father owns an American hotel chain. When they'd married Laura sat in the first row, beamed politely, and thought, *you will never struggle*.

"Just post something," he tells her. "Then it's done with."

"What'll I do about the comments?"

"You just have to post something if you go back on. Otherwise it will be just—It'll be weird. Everybody knows you split up. I mean, Mallory has like three thousand friends. You know?"

"What? What do you mean? Did she post something? What did she post?" Laura, who'd never been very into Facebook, had put an embargo on it since Mallory packed her things and left.

"Okay, okay never mind. Just give me your password. I'll do it."

His youngest, just eight months, screams in the background and the older children sing, "PHONE HE'S ON THE PHONE QUIET QUIET QUIET HE'S ON THE PHONE PHONE PHONE," followed by maniacal pack laughter. Mallory had always said that they should live in the same city. She loved the kids, their insatiable love, how they shoved their fingers into her mouth, tried to unravel her tight curls. After their week-long visits, Laura always spent an evening on the couch, watching music videos or a movie on her laptop, slowly recharging. Mallory had laughed at her: *you're like an old lady*. Mallory, an only child, had lovingly followed and viciously mocked Greg's novelistic Facebook albums of his family. Cherub-faced kid beside a potted rare kind of fern on his cedar deck. "Greg is one step away from Gerber babies," she'd say solemnly. "You need to stop him."

"Won't I have to respond to what people say?" Laura says now.

"You don't have to log in if you don't want to."

But of course she would. She wouldn't be able to resist inputting her name and password, an anagram of Mallory's name and 0703, the anniversary of their first date, coffee and a documentary about penguin migration, which had made Mallory cry on the walk to Laura's car afterwards—"I can't believe how many of them *die*"—and Laura had kept walking, uncomfortable, thinking that she would not call Mallory again, that this woman was just too much for her, too much. So she hadn't answered the first two voicemails Mallory left after that date, both of them five times longer than any message a normal person would leave, Laura had thought, calmly, rationally, pressing Delete.

Username and password, muscle memory. *Raymorlo703*. She is a hacker's dream, these numbers embedded in all of her passwords. Banking, cellphone account, debit and credit PINs, passwords to dating websites she'd secretly cruised for the last few months of their six years together, not out of serious interest but for passive entertainment. *Lots of people must do this*, she'd thought. *It's innocent*. She'd aimlessly browsed the profiles of hopeful women, their open-ended self-descriptions and whimsical profile images. Rosie the Riveter; a panda holding a plate of brownies; a smirking Tina Fey. Half the profiles of people in their twenties used that actress from the TV vampire series Laura can't watch because of the blood—a wan, pastel cheekbone of a woman who isn't even very attractive, her vampire boyfriend cropped out. One woman wrote to her: *We have so much in common, it's like we're meant to be, can I see a photograph?* Laura had deleted the message in a panic, the sounds of Mallory showering after her ride home coming from the bathroom. Mallory had loved her cycle commute across two bridges and along the river. Now driving those bridges Laura looks straight ahead, the bike lane a hard margin against her eyes. The yellow backs with silver stripes. Each one is Mallory.

"Why do I have to say anything?"

Her little brother is silent on the other end of the line.

"If you say nothing," he says finally, "you'll feel worse."

"God, we're all such robots," she breathes heavily.

"If spending time on that thing makes you feel like shit, just don't log in. It's a piece of shit anyway," he adds encouragingly. "Lots of people don't use it. It doesn't matter anyway," he lies. She says goodbye and logs in.

The blue and white blocks, the faces in yearbook arrays. It's all suddenly so incredibly small, the quips and posts, tickets printed with script and hurled to the wind.

Click. Her profile. *Click.*

Her profile photo is a ferry deck shot taken by Mallory—gull origami nighttime flight, wind-slapped cheeks, Laura's hair exploded in a dark swarm. Her stomach twists at how post-coital the photo looks, as if they'd just fucked on the ferry deck against the Pacific-chilled white steel.

Mallory had bellowed over the rushing wind while taking the photo: "Put your arms out. Wider. Wider." Laughter. "Wider."

That smile, no idea what's coming. *You idiot.*

She deletes the photo, fingers popping wild across the keys. Heart absently hammering. Her drink slops onto her leg, just missing her keyboard. The smell of rum spreading down her thigh.

A powder-blue avatar pops up.

A no-her. Statuesque graphic. She can't even erase herself— there will always be another digital stand-in.

She scrolls through her newsfeed. Mallory's endless number of acquaintances, Laura's co-workers whom she sees every day, Mallory's friends from veterinary school, Mallory's friends from her bike racing squad. A few friends from Laura's under-grad, from over a decade ago. But mostly these are Mallory's people. Profiles attached to her by the tentacles of her dead relationship. Where are *her* people?

Laura types into the blue-bordered status box, *Moving on is hard but*

Delete delete delete.

Well they say that

Delete.

The sun will come out tomorrow so smile smile smile

Delete.

Starting a new time in my life, looking forward to the next chapter.

Delete.

You are all going to die alone kids. HAHAHAHAHA!

Delete.

Settings.

Deactivate profile.

Are you sure you want to deactivate your profile?

And then the social networking system taunts her with loneliness, displays photos of her acquaintances, with a repeated message under each face:

Stacey will miss you,
David will miss you,
Leslie will miss you,
Max will miss you,
Matthew will miss you,
Janice will miss you,
Pat will miss you,
Ray will miss you.
Delete.
Click.

⸙

No one really watches the TVs in the gym—five flatscreens set on mute. Laura's weight routine (eight machines, then free weights) overlaps with the daily evening string of game shows.

The subtitles roll past:

[DO YOU WANT
TO TAKE THIS CHANCE
TO INCREASE YOUR
EARNINGS TO ONE
HUNDRED AND FIFTY
THOUSAND DOLLARS?]

The host's face twitches. The camera sweeps the audience.

[AUDIENCE APPLAUSE]

The contestant is in her mid-fifties. She perches in a black blazer with orange piping. She's wearing a taupe headband. *Who wears headbands?*

[WILL YOU TAKE
THIS CHANCE?]
[YES.]

The lights dim to a smoky blue, then dissolve into a white dome.

[SUSPENSEFUL
MUSIC]
[YOU HAVE REACHED
THE NEXT LEVEL
PAMELA.]

The woman spreading backward, legs out, blocky gums and teeth in a close-up.

[AUDIENCE
APPLAUSE]

Laura presses slightly upward. This week, she increased the weights to ninety pounds to see how it would feel. Her muscles climb and ache. The way her lungs feel when she spends slightly too long under water. She holds the weights there, in that place of almost too much.

[YOU'RE MOVING ON
TO THE NEXT LEVEL.
HOW DOES IT FEEL
PAMELA?]
[INCREDIBLE JUST
INCREDIBLE]

Laura can't catch her breath. Mallory loved these shows as much as Laura hated them. "I can't resist the pageantry," Mallory had said. "I love it for the same reason I love Harry Potter!" Laura would leave the room, stand in the kitchen, washing dishes until Mallory came into the kitchen and put her arms around her from behind, whispered into her neck, "Don't hate me because I love the things you hate." She said this about lots of things: Chicken McNuggets meals, documentaries about the British Royal family, malls, dried seaweed, SPCA commercials, cargo shorts, long distance biking. She used to go on daylong rides to Tsawwassen, the town by the ferry terminal, and come back and lie on the dog bed and moan. Laura never understood, watched her, mystified—this exuberant human with whom she happened to split life.

Laura holds the weights away from her body until the sensation shreds through her bared teeth. She could hold it here forever. She lets it back in. Slowly. Draws it back to her chest, lets it bear in hard, lets it press there. Back and ass rooted to the seat of the machine. Opens her legs wide. A feeling glows in her, a hand at the base of her spine. Mallory's voice in her ear: *do you feel that? that's your pelvic floor.* A shudder tumbles through her.

In what bedroom, where had she said this. How many more times, these summonings in her body. Mallory's hand cupping the base of her spine.

She lets the weights go.

They slam down on either side of her ears.

She heaves, staring at the screens. Were there this many competition shows before the economy collapsed? Recession porn. The shows are far-ranging. High school math teachers performing Broadway musical numbers; B-list movie stars paired off and hacking out tangos; a show about a Christian family with twenty children, crewcuts and braids and check-ered shirts. *Why are these people inflicting this on themselves?* Laura thinks. Mallory loved this crap. Especially the Christians, their colonies of offspring, their plans to renovate the double garage to raise more alpacas. *It's a family project! Everybody pitches in!* They are, Laura thinks spitefully, like a Revivalist Chuckie Cheese.

A girl, eleven or twelve, tells the talent show audience that she shares a bed with her single mother, that her father was an alcoholic who beat them. The judges prompt her performance of an old Etta James number.

[THE STAGE IS
YOURS.
IN YOUR OWN
SWEET TIME SWEET
HEART.]

It is easy to stop. This is what she has discovered.

Easy to stop answering email. Easy to come and go from the paperwork at the office, bring nothing and leave nothing behind. Move through the cream and steel lobby, the wax museum of co-workers. So easy to heave off all things. So easy. So easy to write back to Mallory's best friend Jared, *Stop emailing me. I'm not Mallory and you never went out of your way to get to know me*, and delete his responding email without reading it. All things are contracts, not covenants. Easy to say nothing. Easy to stop acknowledging, and then reading, invitations. Easy to not move in relation to others. To amputate herself from gatherings. Mallory, who was a gathering.

⸺⸺⸺

The ultimate test of strength, the trainer had said at the introductory weightlifting class, is to be able to hold up your own weight. Hold yourself aloft. The trainer, a woman in her late fifties, made of thick rope and cantilevered joints, veins exposed. Laura watched her, amazed. Mallory had been the one who exercised, duct-taped an uncle's caving headlamp to her bike before buying the proper gear. Her gear was always left piled by the front door for Laura to throw into the laundry room. Now when Laura opens their front door, she still smells Mallory's sharp sweat, almost reaches for the pile of wet gear.

The automated reminder call for the weightlifting class from the community centre had popped up on their landline voicemail a week after Mallory moved out. Laura hadn't known Mallory had signed up for a weightlifting class. She hadn't known Mallory had any interest in refining her cyclist body, her tendons already violin-tuned. *This message is for Mallory Lee Rhymer*, a voice had recited. *This is a reminder.*

Laura had gone to the class. She'd told herself it was to try something new, but really she had thought Mallory might be there. At the class, a woman in her seventies told them she was there for her osteoporosis. "Turns out my bones aren't what they used to be!" she said cheerfully and the whole group burst into laughter.

The woman at the next locker looks over at Laura. "Good workout?"

"Yeah."

"You were working hard in there."

It had never occurred to Laura that someone could be watching her. But, of course. What else would people do, while lying around grunting? "Thanks."

"How long've you been lifting?"

"Not too long. Couple months, I guess."

"You're pretty solid."

"I think I'm getting there."

Small talk is a way to keep moving. Small talk is a kind of humming. Laura never understood this before—she always wondered at the uselessness of it. For her, cocktail parties and grocery store aisle conversations were exercises in failed lip reading. Mallory had mocked this affectionately: "You just don't understand people at all, do you?" Now she understands.

"I'm George, by the way."

"George?"

"It's short for a name so horrible and ugly I refuse to inflict it on others."

"Georgephine?"

"Oh my god! Nobody's ever guessed before." Laura laughs, zipping up her jeans.

George's hair is shaved close. When she bends to untie and slip off her sneakers, Laura sees that the back of her head is surprisingly flat. *Like a zombie head*, Laura thinks to herself.

"I'm Mallory," Laura says.

George glances up. "Hi, Mallory. Long day?"

"Pretty average."

George nods at her shoes.

"Just a long day at work," Laura says. "Passport office."

"Sounds exciting."

"It is what it is." Laura shrugs and George nods. "The work is not letting people drive you nuts."

"Well, I'm a teacher. When we aren't on strike, we're arguing about going on strike.

George strips quickly. A body that has lifted weights for years. She's probably in her mid-fifties. Something Laura's father told her once—you can tell someone's age by the backs of their hands.

"You're here all the time now, eh?"

"Pretty much every day," Laura says.

George nods, drifting toward the shower, pulling on her flip-flops. "It can get pretty addictive, once you get into it. Nothing better."

Laura drives home, hair damp from her shower, her shoulders and arms injected with honey endorphins. The cyclists pass her, brilliant fish in a parallel stream, their safety jackets smeared across her wet windshield.

At home, it takes an instant to reactivate her Facebook profile. The grid of friends' faces, her truncated history. And then, there is Mallory's face. She's cut her hair short, scooped up around her ears and piled boyishly onto one side, and there is another woman's face in the photo. Their eyes and cheekbones are matching and bright.

Don't click on her. Don't do it. Internet law.

What's on your mind? the status box asks her.

She types in: *The person you most want to see will become the person you least want to see.*

She presses post and logs out.

<hr>

She's getting stronger. A hinged thing. Flesh firm around her joints, her shoulders suddenly, one day, blade-like.

Laura has watched her body in the mirrored wall in the gym, watched her body change. Her neck plunges into her collarbone. When she turns and looks at her back in her bedroom mirror, it is a raised plateau. Her outside layer has peeled away. She remembers those anatomical models from high school biology class, human puzzles, their removable spleens.

The men at the gym now call her *bro*. One day, a shrug-nod and then, coolly, *hey, bro.* The luck of broad shoulders. Her new bro status pleases her in spite of herself. She moves the pin in the weights to one hundred and twenty pounds. Midlift, she looks at her right arm, the new tough packet resting there. When she felt the new muscle for the first time, her mind flooded with worry: *a lump*. Her mind looks for reasons to panic everywhere. No, this is what she's been working for—this hardness. Beside her, a man strains on the piece of equipment dubbed the birthing machine. Weights attach to pads placed against the inside of each thigh. He squeezes and releases. *Aaaaahhhhhhhhhhhhhh*. Laura ties her shoelace to conceal her smirk.

The woman, possibly a dancer, who balances on the exercise bench every night. One arm extended. A weight at the end of her arm, muscle a perfect arc, a soft band. Laura watches. The pure control of motionlessness.

———∞∞∞———

She logs in and the cursor flashes at her, asking her to fill in the box. *What's on your mind?*, the pale blue text taunts her, flashes, implores her.

She types in: *You are the only one pretending to be you.*

———∞∞∞———

There are people and their ways of moving. There are the storks and the straight-necked and the sufferers, backs bent, ears blocked out by the steel orbiting rings. The men who strut the length of the floor. The men who supervise the shapes of their muscles in the mirrored wall, sleeves summoned upright. How could anyone who goes to a gym think that women are the vain sex? Late at night, rows of men's hands wrap the metal bars. One man, compact and anguished, paces to the water fountain after every set of repetitions.

Another guy guides his body through cycle after cycle on the leg press, extends and withdraws, pumping the bellows of a great machinery. Laura feels it occasionally as she lifts—a roughness in her blood. She has realized that her muscles have their own busy lives. Sometimes when she pulls on the weights, there is an absence there; sometimes, there is a humming, a throbbing, begun before she makes her demand. Laura ignores these quiet pulses, learns to pull with the same force every time.

—∞—

When she tells Greg about the weightlifting, she makes sure to slip it in casually at the tail end of one of their phone calls, but he stops and his voice lowers on the other end of the line. "Whoa whoa whoa, what?"

"Weightlifting," she says.

"That's awesome. How long? What?"

"Pretty much every day."

A long pause. "Since Mallory left?"

"Yeah, pretty much."

"Well, that's great, Lo, that's great, that's really great, good for you. I mean, I'm really glad you found an outlet." He pauses, waiting for her to say more, and pushes, "So, is it helping?"

"What's that supposed to mean?"

"I mean, you've been having a hard time. Dad called me. He says you don't answer any of his emails or phone messages."

"That's because all of his emails and phone messages are about kale."

"Lo. Look. We all know what she did is pretty fucking terrible. I mean, who fucking—who just *leaves* like that? But, I mean, you two were always—"

"Always what?"

"Nothing, it's just—"

"Always what?"

His voice goes whiny, like it always does when he knows he's losing. But he can't stop. That's the thing about him; he just never knows when to stop. "Well, you know as well as anyone. You two were always so different. I mean, I guess, I always thought. She was just so much *louder*. You know?" Then he says the worst thing. "Maybe it's better this way." He breathes and says, "Anyway, Dana says to come here for as long as you need, the kids want to see you and? They want to see you." He waits. "I want to see you. Do you see anybody?"

By the time she makes a pot of Roiboos tea and checks her email he's already sent her links to articles cautioning against daily weightlifting for women. *You just never know when to stop do you, little brother?* She scans the cautionary paragraphs: not enough testosterone to build muscle as quickly as tissue breaks down, the websites inform her. She clicks on a link in a sidebar to an album of female bodybuilders; she scans for the dykes, scrolls through the stomach muscles and linebacker shoulders, sipping her cooled orange pekoe, the tears rivering down her cheeks. Everybody had known. Everybody had seen but her. And this is the part she cannot tell anyone, even Greg—she does not understand why Mallory left, cannot explain it to anybody, how Mallory raged at her that things had been off for a year and she'd had no idea, how could she have known nothing at all. She texts Greg: I feel so old.

⸺ ❈ ⸺

She's among the last ones there at night. This small group, buff stragglers. A staffer flickers the lights; library manners.

Laura blasts her body with scalding water in the showers, the steam pressing cloud formations against the walls, her knuckles tense. She checks her shoulders. A faint string of burst blood vessels again. Is this how it starts, she wonders, people who get into pain? Backslide, wander, trip into it. *No, I'm not like that. I'm not one of those people.* When she pulls the towel around her body, her skin is red. The burst blood vessels stand out in dark purple, a kitchen tattoo. She checks her right shoulder and, yes, there's the string of erupted blood vessels. Tonight, the damage reassures her.

In the locker room, the last women are half-naked, benches draped with yoga pants and rain jackets. While she dresses, Laura cannot help but inspect the other women's marks and scars. The tattoos. Laura would never get a tattoo. Too permanent. In undergrad, her roommate got a tattoo after she got a call from home that her childhood dog had been run over by a car. The tattoo was her dog's licence number, printed across the back of her neck. "You look like you have a bar code," Laura had told her, surprised when her roommate had burst into tears and rushed from the room, then for the rest of the term communicated with Laura only through Post-It notes. Mallory had leaned forward and whispered with a kind of awe, "Oh my god, I think that's the most insensitive thing I've actually ever heard. You're *amazing*." Laura had never been able to tell whether Mallory was making fun of her or praising her.

Both and more.

Long-term rented lockers are decorated with family photographs. Mallory would have made Laura rent a locker, stock it with protein bars. Her thoughtfulness could be controlling. "I'm kind of insidious," she had once told Laura proudly, and Laura had thought, *I want that.*

"Hey, Mallory."

Laura looks up from unhooking her bra, shocked, to see George, her mild smile, and, startlingly, missing a tooth.

It's too late to correct her about the name. And, she realizes, she speaks to so few people these days that not being called by her own name isn't even really very surprising.

"Hello, Georgephine."

"Smoke?"

"Seriously?"

"Yeah. Seriously."

Outside the building, they lean against the brick wall.

"It's so *warm*," she says and George laughs.

"You never smoked before?"

"Just not for a long time."

"Ah. I see."

"I've smoked."

"Sure you have." George smokes evenly, perfectly. "Anyway, look at you, the dedicated gym bunny and I'm ruining your perfect health." Laura smiles into the darkness. It's been a long time since anyone has flirted with her.

"Gym bunny. Ha."

"Seems like you're here even more than I am."

"It's just recent."

"Is it? Lifting?"

"Yeah and even the gym. I'd actually never been in a gym before."

"Really?" George's muscular body is a lean shadow in the dimness. "What made you go from zero to sixty?"

Laura hesitates. "Just a stupid breakup."

"Ah. Bad?"

"Yeah."

"Ah." George throws her cigarette at her foot, grinds it slowly. "Well, then, that makes a lot of sense, Mallory."

"What?" Laura's neck snaps to the side. "What's that supposed to mean?"

"The way you lift. You know, like you've got something to prove."

Laura stares at George's profile but sees no hint of satisfaction—just her mouth set and calm, as if she's just read out the price of an item for sale. After a few minutes of silence, Laura realizes that George isn't going to say anything more. She leans back into the wall and watches traffic. Rain begins to fall, hooks at her lip.

⌘

The streets are dark, empty. Houses and houses and houses, stuffed with their hosts. The weights made tunnels in her. Dug her up again. She will go home again to the empty condo.

A white fish cruises along the side of the dark road.

The bicycle drifts in its lane.

Laura swerves slightly.

The cyclist jerks, bends outward, pulled by the magnet in the centre of Laura's driver's wheel.

She swerves gently again, hears the bellow of surprise from the cyclist this time, how she can press herself gently into him.

She swerves again, comes back to centre.

His yell comes clear through the glass: "CRAZY FUCKING BITCH."

This time she slows down as she swerves. Looks across the passenger seat and sees the cyclist's face. Not the hardened urban cyclist she'd expected but a teenaged boy clinging to the handlebars like a tree branch he's climbed too far out on. His fearful hunch, face angled across his neck, eyes stretched wide.

She swerves one more time and watches him go over into the ditch.

⎯⎯ ∞∞ ⎯⎯

When she gets home, she huddles in her bed, the whole quilt around her body. Her body shivers so hard her knees knock against her chest. She pulls her laptop from the bedside table, opens it, and there's her Facebook page.

She types in: *your body was my home.* She presses post. Sucks in her breath when she sees the words float there.

Hurriedly clicks her cursor in the blank space again.

Types in: *it isnt over if theres nothing left something was there then nothing*

Post. A tiny red 1 appears in the top right corner of her screen. She doesn't recognize the name of the person who liked her first post. Her body is still so cold.

Another blank space and she fills it in: *breaking open*

Another blank space.

She types: *nighttimes are worst when you sleep alone every night you feel alone all day you go back every time*

She types: *you planned it for so long and i had no idea. HOW.* Post.

She types: *this is so poignant are you watching?*

She types: *can a person actually just fall in love with a cypher?*

She types: *blood vessels break down very easily did you know I didnt.* Post.

She clicks the white camera icon to take a selfie. There she is, shockingly lean. Eyes large, the strong arch of one arm, the muscles visible. She clicks and the selfie stabilizes, both unfocused and luminous. A stranger gazes back at her from her new profile picture, jaw set, unmoving. The image pops up beside each of the posts, a row of her, shrunken and staring, beside her words, the only true words she has spoken since Mallory left. Sleep takes her down.

❦

She prefers the gym late at night. The bodies and wheels. The low hum. The feeling of this day, and that day, and the next, and the next, entering and leaving her flesh. Her limbs pressed into rotations deepening their paths. Joints; grindstones. Her breath under one hundred pounds, two hundred pounds. The soft hammer against the front of her throat, marking out time. She is so strong now. Stronger than she has ever been. People rise and move from one machine to the next, busy with their private reasons for hardening.

Every day parts of her shift and tighten. Parts of her slacken. Laura presses herself until her bones bloom, her arms arc and make more room for more blood. There are gulfs and channels in her body, open spaces she has never known before. She enters them.

J.R. McCONVEY

HOME RANGE

She is tiny and thin, maybe six, wearing a white blouse smudged with grease and oil, and a navy skirt that barely covers her scraped knees. When Kyle hauls up the door she's just standing there like a curious bird, dead still, echoes of the metal's clang circling her like nervous black cats half hidden in the shadows. The sight of her inside the container, amid the stacked pallets and crates, the smells of wet tin and briny mildew, is like a lullaby lilted over a pounding hardcore beat, incongruous and adorable and unsettling as hell.

It takes Kyle three seconds to realize he can't tell anyone about the girl, five to figure out he can't just leave her there, ten to know how fucked he is as a result. Fifteen to write it off as just more of the cursed luck that's his trademark, as much a totem of his being as the sleeve tattoos that fill both his arms from shoulder to wrist with a chaos of thorny blue vines.

He looks around the empty pier. The Atlantic sloshes and trickles, chewed around its edges by the croaking of gulls and the grinding of heavy machinery behind him. Pier 17 is out on the far edge of the wharf, many rows of lots away from the main office and the warehousing deck. It's just him and his forklift and the sludge of trash and seaweed slapping the breaker wall. And the girl. Japanese, maybe. No. More likely poorer, easier to make disappear. Thai or Malaysian, something like that. Fuck knows. Wherever she's come from, she's far from home, and Kyle is willing to bet his signed vinyl copy of *Jane Doe* that the trip wasn't her choice.

He curses in his head, cycling through options at blastbeat pace, *whattodowhattodowhattodo*.

"Speak English?" he says. No response. "Name? What's your name?" The girl just looks at him, head cocked to one side, hiding with felted calm whatever explosions of terror and confusion must be raging in her brain like Bengal flares.

"Fuck," he says to no one. The wind tickles his nose with gull shit, wood rot, and tar slag. In the distance he hears the bleating reverse alarm of another forklift, the harmonic whirr of the hydraulic elevator. Even out here at 17, he has ten, maybe fifteen minutes before someone drives by, fellow grunt or foreman, to ask what the fuck is taking him so long with the shipment from Kwai Tsing.

In the end it's maybe a two-minute decision, based on what's immediately available, proximity to the parking lot, number of hours left in his shift. All instinct, like the survival games he used to play as a kid. If there's anything Kyle can say he's good at, it's surviving.

There's a big roll of brown packing paper leaning against a nearby stack of crates. He gestures to the girl: *Come out.* She steps slowly from the container, blinking in the salt mist. Kyle notices the bruising on her arms. She probably spent her trip through the Suez cowering back into a far corner of the container. Maybe did the same when it was opened in Amsterdam. Someone there made sure she knew better than to try to hide when the door was opened the next time.

He wonders what she's been eating, if he should check the interior for evidence—wrappers, crumbs, some kind of bed. Not that it matters. Whoever shipped her knows which lot she's in, will have carefully traced its route from HK to 17. There's no way she could have gotten this far without a network of people making it happen. Valuable cargo, this.

It's a freak chance, a big mistake, that Kyle's the one here on the receiving end. So he doesn't have time to work out the consequences: it has to be fast, brutal, full-on punk rock. Instinct over thought.

Maybe, he thinks for the millionth time, he isn't done with all that yet. Maybe he can save her.

Drawing out a large swath of the paper, he wraps it round the girl, placing his hand gently on the crown of her head to keep her still and try to communicate that he's trying to help, until she's just an inconspicuous brown sausage, another bit of material piled on the back platform of his Caterpillar. He makes sure she's on her back, has a slit to breathe through. Does what he can to tell her to keep still. She gives no pushback. Before folding the flap down over her head to hide her slick of smooth black hair, he leans in and whispers to her, shitting his pants, patting his chest, "Friend. Friend. Home. My home. *Konichiwa?*" A bit of packing tape and she's invisible.

Hour and a half until quitting. Finish your tasks, don't look anyone in the face, park the lift, haul her out like an old carpet or a bit of excess wrap for dumping, throw her in the back seat of the pickup, drive home without speeding, get her inside. Between now and then, he figures, he can sort out what the fuck he's going to tell Abby.

They sit on the worn turquoise carpet, playing. Most of Abby's dolls have missing limbs and torn clothes, but she still manages to craft amazing mini-luxe fantasies with them: shopping, eating at nice restaurants, driving around astride the old Tonka truck Kyle picked up at the Sally Ann. The language barrier is less of a problem for kids. The Asian girl—he's resisted giving her a name—took no time to warm up to the dolls. She obviously knows Barbie. She and Abby are busy placing them in pairs, with their thin plastic legs stretched out, feet touching.

He thinks how much Krista would have loved this. She always said she wanted two.

It will be six years in November. It'd be impossible to forget anyway, but the anniversary coming a day after Abby's birthday always makes for a particularly hard emotional thrashing. He still has trouble believing it. Sepsis doesn't seem like a thing that should kill people, not in this country, not in this age. Not at barely twenty-three years old, with enough brass to tell a roomful of rich old men in Armani suits that they're vassals of the patriarchy, even while they sneer at your bleached hair and piercings. Kris had already been through hell by the time she met Kyle—touchy father, drunk mom, more than a few winter nights sleeping on the street. That she'd managed to pull herself up, find the strength to help others through her work at the shelter—it was a miracle. She only got the one, though. Unless you also count Abby, the child she knew for a day and a half. Kris never even made it home from the hospital.

The girls are keeping busy for now, so Kyle gives himself a minute to sit on the couch and work up a plan. Normally he'd put on a record to help him think, *I Against I* or *Monuments to Thieves*, but he doesn't want to scare the new girl with the vicious noise he loves. Instead he turns on the TV and clicks around until he finds a station rerunning *The Shawshank Redemption*. Vanilla as it is, Kyle has a soft spot for the movie. He'd convinced his old band, Pinched Nerve, to name a song after it—"Andy Dufresne." Krista had always loved that one, made sure to come up close to the stage whenever they played it, to watch him shred through the blitzkrieg chorus: *"He says there's no memory / I want to live what's left of my life / In a warm place / Without memory."* Her smiling, arms raised, screaming along with him, feeling the same ache.

He'll have to keep the girl here for tonight, at least. He knows it can't go much beyond that. An orphanage, maybe? The thought chills him, all wrought iron beds and sadistic nurses and gruel. Besides, what's he going to do—leave her on the doorstep tied with ribbon? Rewrap her in the packing paper and call it an early Christmas parcel? He wants her to be safe, protected, but there can't be anything linking her to him. With the band long finished, the wharf is his lifeline now. Abby will be starting school next fall . . . which means books, clothes, backpacks. Things to pay for.

He opens a couple cans of Beef-a-Roni for the girls and gives them another hour or so before taking them together into the washroom. Abby picks up her toothbrush and squirts on a blob of bubblegum-flavoured toothpaste.

"Daddy, is it okay if Soo-bin and I share?" she says.

For a second he hears *soy bean*. Then he realizes. Winces. Nods his head.

"Yes, sweetie."

The girl—Soo-bin—takes the brush, touches it to the stream of water gurgling from the tap, runs it back and forth across her little Chiclet teeth, curious and mute. He wonders how much of this is new to her, what kind of conditions she lived in back home. He wonders if she feels lucky that Kyle found her. He wonders if she is.

Once the girls are asleep, he sits down in front of *Shawshank* with a can of Pabst to decompress. He goes through the exercises his mother taught him after Kris died: start with the eyes. Then the jaw. Move down through the neck and shoulders . . . let relaxation fall over your joints like dandelion wisps. He still finds himself fighting it—answering every loosening with a desire to grit teeth, grip mic, bark a righteous retort. Pummel stress into submission. Live hardcore as a steady inner scream. There's no one to scream at, though. Just Red and Andy Dufresne, and why would he scream at them. He swigs beer, savouring the sour aluminum fizz. Closes his eyes, trying to feel the warm place.

Kris, massaging his shoulders after a show. Working the strained muscle, popping a joint into his mouth from behind, holding it for him while he inhales.

Over the droning of the TV, he hears a dull thump outside. His eyes pop open. The girl? He gets up, drains his beer, and goes over to peer through the half-open door to Abby's room. Two bundles snuggle each other on the bed, rising and falling with children's breath. Safe, both. He turns back to the movie, where Andy Dufresne is counting seconds between thunderclaps. Kyle doubts anyone from the wharf would come for him at night. Not worth the effort, when you can intimidate someone just as well in the light of day.

He hears the hollow clunk again. Recognizes tactile, insistent scratching. This part of town is a magnet for raccoons. They must be at the garbage, rooting for old apple cores and cheese-caked pizza boxes. He grabs the broom and another Pabst and snaps the porch light on before stepping out into the foggy grey night.

Crouched comfortably on its haunches, nibbling away at the remains of an old corn cob, the fat masked invader squats in front of an upturned compost bin and turns its head toward Kyle: *What? What you gonna do?* Kyle waves the broom around a few times, smacks it on the paint-chipped porch slats. He knows it's futile. These things have no fear, will sit there ransacking your trash right in front of you unless you take drastic measures. Kyle's never had the heart. Krista volunteered at the humane society and would always come home with horror stories about coons full of buckshot, or choking their way through the last throes of death by Javex-brined chicken carcass. For the most part, he's learned to live with them, clean up their toxic feces during the day, and hope they end up moving on to another bin once they've cleaned out the meagre leavings in his.

Besides, Kyle and the raccoons go back a ways. He remembers a night his grandfather let him help set the traps. Nonlethal—just a bit of peanut butter bait and a trigger-action wire-mesh door that would hold them until morning, when Granddad would load the cage in the back of his pickup and drive them outside the city limits to let them free. Kyle wanted to know why they couldn't just put them in the neighbour's yard.

"Thing about raccoons," said his grandfather. "They know where they live. Know their territory. You gotta take 'em an hour out at least, go out beyond their home range. Otherwise, they'll just come back."

Kyle stares at the big mangy guy gnawing the cob like an old man chewing on a pipe stem. He wonders if this critter has been here before. If he recognizes Kyle—knows that this thin, wiry ex-punk with the two-day stubble and bramble tats is no threat to him. Kyle can smell his musk, the sour stink of old fish and muddy water. The raccoon keeps nibbling, eyes cast sideways at Kyle, waiting for him finally to get angry and take a real swing with the broom.

Kyle turns and goes inside and turns off the porch light. White credits crawl up the black screen, hundreds of names disappearing as they crest the dusty curve of his old tube TV. Kyle clicks off the remote and the room plunges into darkness. He listens, for a minute, to make sure he can still hear the girls breathing, before going into his bedroom and collapsing into his unmade bed with his jeans still on.

The knock comes at 10 a.m., as the girls are tucking into their Quaker Instant Maple Brown Sugar oatmeal. Even though he's been waiting for it, Kyle flinches like he's been stuck with a shiv up under the ribs. He spent all night thinking, trying to sort out what to do with the girl—with Soo-bin. But he just kept coming back to Andy Dufresne, hammering on his sewage pipe in the darkness, and to Krista, lying on the hospital bed, the berserking metronome of the heart monitor shocking her life into the terrible flatline that took all of Kyle's rage and pinched it into the helpless scream of a newborn. And to Abigail, *his daughter, his daughter, his daughter*, the word so charged with joy and pain that it still explodes, every time he thinks it, like a bomb inside the inner chambers of his scar-worn heart.

The next knock comes, more insistent than the first. He gets up and gives himself maybe thirty seconds to haul Soo-bin up out of her kitchen chair, shushing Abby to quell her hurt questioning look, and hauls the cargo girl into his bedroom, where he stuffs her into the closet and puts all the compassion he has into his eyes and mumbles an apologetic plea—*justaminutepleasebequietjustaminute*—before piling an old Slayer hoodie on top of her and closing the door and heading back out to answer to whoever it is that wants her back. As he grips the knob, Kyle puts on his calmest face, thinking how natural it will be to pretend that the second bowl of Quaker is for himself, hoping for the absurd impossibility that somehow, instead of someone from the union, it's the raccoon from last night come knocking to ask him for another corn cob or to apologize for the awkward standoff they'd found themselves in during the midnight raid.

"Mr. Miller. Good morning."

Kyle's fantasy falls away as soon as he opens the door and sees Szandor Zabados, head of the local ILA chapter, standing there with his cigarette pinched daintily between thumb and forefinger, shoulders hunched into his thick khaki coat, eyes gleaming oily crow-black under a thinning fringe of copper-pipe hair. Kyle has seen Szandor berate his fair share of stevedores, but that's just the tip of it. Rumours have him deeply involved in trafficking, graft, and pedophilia, and they're the kind of rumours everyone knows are true. Zabados keeps one can of Diet Pepsi per day in the staff refrigerator, and Kyle can remember the day some rookie decided to drink it and ended up getting a pink slip and a six-foot-five, 270-pound escort to the parking lot, who made it crystal clear that any further appearance at the wharf would result in a dislocated jaw and the distinct possibility of an indelicately removed testicle.

"Szandor?" Kyle says, feigning surprise, trying to channel his old performer's instincts. "Surprised to see you on my porch on a Saturday morning. Can I do for you?"

Zabados takes a drag of his cigarette and looks long ways down the street, in the direction of the ocean.

"You want to come in?" says Kyle, stepping slightly to the side, hoping to hell the answer is no.

"I got a bit of a problem, Miller," Zabados says. "Maybe you can help me."

"Sure."

"You were on 17 yesterday, yeah?"

"That's right."

Zabados looks him in the eye, a barrel of smouldering ash clinging to the tip of his butt.

"I know it is. I know you were on 17."

Kyle manages a curious frown. "What's the problem?"

"You see anything unusual on your shift?"

"No . . . can't say I did."

"Can't say? Or . . . ?"

Kyle tries to summon saliva into his mouth, which suddenly feels coated with cement.

"I honestly don't know what you're getting at. Sorry to disappoint. Yesterday was a pretty standard shift."

Zabados chucks his smoke onto the worn planks of Kyle's porch, not far from the dark smears left from the raccoon's marauding. He shoves his hands deep into his pockets, looks back down the road, presenting Kyle with a gnarled cauliflower ear veined through with red blood vessels.

"All right, Miller," he says. "Just remember. The union's here to take care of you. I know you like your days off to spend with your daughter."

Kyle says nothing.

"Be sure to let me know if you hear anything on the wharf, yeah?"

"Okay, Szandor. Will do."

"Me, I'm gonna go get some lunch. Great little Korean place up near Fairmount," he says. "You like Korean?"

For a minute Kyle is confused, thinks his trollish foreman might actually be asking him out for a meal.

"I love it," Zabados says. "Even that kimchi. Smells like an old sock. You gotta watch the spice, though. You're not careful, it can wreak havoc on your insides."

The implication jabs a stinger at Kyle's brain, prodding for the name that's suddenly shaking inside him like a trembling kitten: *Soo-bin.*

Like, Korean, Kyle?

Zabados turns to go but stops and twists his head around, demon-style, at the bottom of Kyle's steps.

"Anything pops into your head, anyone call you with something to talk about, you remember—the union takes care of you." He fishes in his pocket, pulls out a flattened pack of Kools, draws one out, and starts tapping it on the inside of his wrist. "Remember that."

"Will do, Szandor."

"See you at work."

Kyle watches Szandor Zabados get into his big black Escalade, shut the door, and drive off in the opposite direction of Fairmount, most likely back to the wharf, to retrieve his cold Pepsi from its voodooed shelf in the staff fridge. He thinks about what's in his own closet, about Abby and her oatmeal, the other bowl cold and congealing beside her. He thinks about Andy Dufresne, keeping his eye on the warm place with no memory. And he thinks about Krista, because he's always thinking about her.

"Where are you going, Daddy?"

The question scuttles back and forth across the dome of his skull, mewling. Abby had known something was weird, of course: Saturdays were their together day, the one put aside to forget bank accounts and old music and dead mothers and the clawing of steamer exhaust in the back of your throat. When he'd taken Abby next door to Mrs. Coover's to plead the favour of watching her for a couple hours, his daughter had been smart or scared enough not to mention Soo-bin. He'd told Abby that he was going to help the girl get home, and she'd accepted that. But she'd still required some answer for his absence, a good reason for his leaving her with the neighbour on a Saturday evening.

The truth would have meant nothing to her. Wharton State Forest, just north of Atlantic City, isn't somewhere she knows. In fact, it's far enough in the wrong direction that Kyle hopes it's a place she'll never end up. He tries not to pressure Abby, to be patient and careful with her. But he's definitely pointing her outside the state—across the river, maybe. Or even farther, to a more civil country. If he has any say in the matter, the whole south shore of New Jersey will exist outside her universe, just not something she'll have to live with, not the way he does.

The Korean girl—North Korean, is Kyle's guess, almost a ghost to begin with—shifts in the driver's seat, staring out the window at the strip malls and industrial parks running along the edge of the turnpike. The cabin smells of stale coffee and sweat and Cheetos and Armor All, which together Kyle processes as the reek of his own helplessness and guilt.

Wharton is big, big enough for someone to get lost in. To go unnoticed. But also a place, maybe, where someone small but resourceful might find a way to survive. It's only the beginning of November. Kyle's leaving Soo-bin with Abby's Barbie parka from last season—a bit tight but warm—some plaid galoshes, a pair of track pants, and an old sweater of Krista's that's big enough for her to wrap around herself like a blanket. To eat, a bunch of bananas, a couple packages of Fig Newtons, and a thermos of instant hot chocolate. It's a far cry from a proper wilderness-survival kit, but surely better than what Szandor Zabados has planned for her.

He couldn't bring himself to call the cops. One way or the other, they'd just bring it back to Zabados. If Kyle was honest with himself, he's already, technically, kidnapped the girl. What else might they say he'd done? What horrible mix of tar and feathers and bird shit could they smear all over him? The orphanage appears in his head again, rows of metal-frame beds and hard-edged shadows, but this time it's Abby standing there, dressed in a grey smock, surrounded by faceless orphans. Her mother dead. Her father convicted. Maybe dead, too.

He's trying. Trying so hard. With the Chef Boyardee and the oatmeal and the thrift store dolls. Processed shit, material shit—the kind of shit he used to rage against. It's all he can afford now, though. You make sacrifices. Kyle wants Abby to have a good life with him, and a decent shot at a better one down the road. He can't shatter that chance. Not for anyone. Not after what he promised.

In the hospital, Krista's just lying there. The oxygen mask makes it hard for Kyle to hear her and there's a noise in his head like a thousand bands slamming through a frenzied breakdown, all shredded vocal cords and shrill guitar and relentless kick-drum hammering. He's squeezing Kris's hand, hard, but his other hand is up on her forearm, wrapped around the blue ring of barbed wire tattooed on her bicep, not squeezing as tightly there because he can sense that her flesh is fragile. Abby is with the nurses. There will be a little more time for mother and daughter to be in the same room— they've promised her that—but the doctors don't like having the baby in the ICU. Kris has already had one kidney fail. They've stopped telling him she'll get better.

She's made it clear that she needs him to listen carefully. It's hard for her to talk now, so Kyle leans in and puts his ear over the cup of the oxygen mask.

"You have to promise," she whispers, a cracked cymbal rasp, shattered and terrified and brave, so brave. "You'll take care of her."

"I will," Kyle says, shaking. "I promise." He can't imagine how he'll do this without Krista. He can't believe what's happening. He can't believe he can't save her. The bands explode in his head into a final pummelling unison and he recognizes the opening bars of "Last Light," first song proper on Converge's *You Fail Me*, his favourite track on the record, which he's been listening to a lot lately.

"Always," Kyle says, his voice breaking. *Our daughter.*

"It's going to mean giving up some things," Kris says.

"I know," he says, blood clanging in his ears, a righteous screaming wounded animal roar. "I know."

He turns onto a road that winds up through wooded slopes. The trees are thick on either side. The lake is just up around the bend about two hundred yards. He pulls over into a clearing, kills the engine and the headlights. The air is crisp and clean and there's a faint scent of wood smoke on the wind and a burbling brook nearby. He climbs out, his breath steaming in the cold, and opens the back door. He unbuckles her seatbelt and steps back and—hating himself for it— waves his hand.

"C'mon, Soo-bin."

She climbs out into the night, boots crunching on the browning leaves.

He squats and looks her in the eyes—big eyes, dark as tea in a black cup. There are fortunes there, tellings beyond what he has talent to read. This, finally, is his problem: What else can he do for her? How does she fit? How is she at all comprehensible? The truth—*I want to save her, she reminds me of my daughter, but I can't, I can't risk it because she is not my daughter*—is too banal, too horrible for Kyle to contemplate. Justice? Where? In what universe does she get handed over to anyone else, anyone good, and not draw all kinds of attention, some politician using her as a campaign platform, some cynical commentator preaching the girl as a harbinger of moral decay? How does that not all boil down to himself and to Abby?

And does Soo-bin even end up any better off? In what scenario is she most likely to be free, really free, for as long as possible?

Kyle can give her the chance to run. To adapt. It's the best act of mercy he can manage.

He's cycling through all this, tattooed arms perched on burning thighs, when she turns and goes. Just starts walking toward the trees, as if she's saving him the trouble of anguishing over it. There's purpose in her walk as she strides away in Abby's plaid boots and Barbie parka. A certain grace. He supposes she understands that she might as well get comfortable. Kyle watches and listens, half expecting the girl to dissolve into the evening mist before his eyes.

At the edge of the trees, though, she stops. For a second Kyle wonders if he's got it wrong—if she'll turn around and run back at him and make him say it out loud, needing to understand his tone even if she doesn't know the English words: *I'm leaving you here.*

Instead, she pulls off the parka and lets it fall down around her ankles in a marshmallowy pink heap. He's about to protest, when he sees it: the bushy striped tail hanging unmistakably from the base of her spine, protruding just above the hem of her track pants. For a distended second, it wavers like a lazy pendulum—then, answering his disbelief, twitches, a quick flick, as if to cast a spell. Soo-bin turns and gives him a curious look, black eyes rimmed with coal-dark smudge. Kyle opens his mouth to speak—say, *What are you?* say, *I used to be better*— but before he can utter a word she's darted off into the trees, the crackle of broken twigs prickling his ears, the grey spirit of a split moon hovering over the treeline.

Kyle squats there on the wet, rotting leaves, taking in the dense weave of branches from behind a blur of tears. Krista's voice murmuring something soft, something about Andy Dufresne and the warm place, he hauls himself up to get back into the truck and crank some hardcore as loud as it will go— loud enough to blot out the cracking in her voice, the smell of her sickness, the flick of the cargo girl's tail, and whatever other echoes haven't fled him yet, even though he knows the music will never work that way again.

CARLEIGH BAKER

CHINS AND ELBOWS

At 5 a.m., Lara and I are on the beach in Port Moody. The morning mist is sea salt and oil slick. Cold waves slap the shore. It's a groggy, rubber-boot clomp to the beat-up aluminum boat at the end of the dock. Lara volunteers with Nature's Little Helpers. Spawning season means it's time for an egg take in Mossom Creek.

"Triple Americano, black. Right?" Lara thrusts a travel mug at me. "It's good to see you." Behind her, a block of beige beach condos disappears into the fog.

"Do we have to kill the fish?" My hands warm around the mug. I won't tell her I've spent every day since I got home drinking decaf. Playing video games. Running a pale, thin elf warrior around a shimmery forest on her horse, killing monsters with a bow. Good versus evil is such a comfort sometimes.

"Oh God, no," Lara says. "Well, somebody does. We'll do other jobs." She worked with Nature's Little Helpers all summer, planting eelgrass along the shoreline, tramping around in the muck like a kid. She wrote me letters about it, each one an invitation to come back to the city. I'd intended to write her back.

The salmon enhancement crew are pony-tailed retirees who probably urban pole to the grocery store. Wheatgrass drinkers. Gulf Island beachfront owners. They hug Lara like old friends and look deep into my eyes when we shake hands. Weird. Seven of us crawl in, hunched over our hot drinks. Smell of boat gas and fish guts.

A woman with a grass-fed complexion and long white hair takes my hand in both of hers.

"Carmen, I'm Diane. Thanks for coming out with us." She turns to Lara. "We'll meet the gals from Alouette Correctional at the river. It's a small crew today."

"That's fine, Carmen can do the work of ten inmates." Lara grins at me, flexes a lean bicep.

"Inmates?" I look at Lara, who looks at Diane.

"Didn't Lara tell you? They send us volunteers during spawning season." Diane is still holding my hand. She squeezes a little before she gives it back.

Up the Burrard Inlet in a tin can. Past freighters and trawlers and pleasure craft. Most years Vancouver stays green, but there's fresh powder on the mountaintops. When I left Prince George three weeks ago, snow was already dusting the downtown streets.

"How was the honey farm?" Lara asks. I have to lean in to hear her over the thrum of the outboard.

"It was hard labour. Heavy lifting. Sweeping dead bees into the drain every night," I say. Her eyes narrow.

"I thought they didn't hurt the bees."

"They were at the end of their productive cycle," I say, mimicking the beekeeper's gruff monotone. "Probably true, but it felt like killing off my co-workers."

"That's awful." Lara lowers her voice. "But you're clean now, right?"

"Three months clean." Saying it like that makes it seem like I've been dirty.

"I knew you'd do it," Lara says. The first hug in a long time is always all chins and elbows.

To everyone except Lara, my trip up north just looked like a weird working holiday. A detox centre would have made it official. So instead I bottled honey, swept and hosed the sticky cement floors clean at Sunny Valley Apiary. The beekeeper wasn't sure about me, half-blood city girl with skinny arms and gaunt cheeks. Shaking and sweating for the first few weeks, until the last of the meth had burned from my lymph. Crying over dead bees. Not surprisingly, there weren't a lot of other people who wanted the job, so I got to stay.

We watch an otter skim along the water, belly up. Something in his paws—looks like a plastic baby toy. He dips under, leaving his loot at the surface. Farther up the inlet it's crab traps and prawn traps and fish nets. Then only water, shore, sky.

Alouette Correctional Centre is on the South Alouette River in Maple Ridge. Lara tells me they just built a new maximum security wing, with little windows in each cell, above the bunks. The windows look out onto medium security, so the women can see how good their well-behaved cell sisters have it. If the maximum security inmates behave, they can join in on community projects: horticulture or doggie daycare or this one, salmon enhancement.

As we approach the dock, Diane points to a tall First Nations woman smoking a cigarette on the shore. Just her and a grim-faced prison guard.

"I'd expected more, but maybe it's just as well," Diane says. "This is the first time we've had a violent offender." *Violent offender* gets finger quotes. The boat bumps against the dock as our wake catches up with us.

"I'm sure it's no biggie," Lara says. "Right, Carmen?"

"Sure." It's annoying to be included in this conversation, like I know anything about violent offenders. I suspect Lara's invited me on this trip as some kind of teachable moment—the ghost of Christmas future—and that's not fair. It's not like I was street hustling. And I stopped using on my own volition. A detox centre would have been cushier, but it might not have been punishment enough. Some mistakes have to be beaten out.

Diane gives the guard the two-handed squeeze. "This is Lucy," the guard says to us, nodding at her charge.

"Lucky," the woman says, stomping out a cigarette. She's wearing a numbered sweatsuit; powder-blue prison casual.

Diane hands her a jar with some water in the bottom. "I'll get you to keep your butts in there today, can't have the fish eating them." She turns back to us without waiting for an answer. "Let's go, everyone." Behind her, Lucky digs three butts out of the sand and drops them in the jar.

Climb from the boat to the back of a fisheries pickup, and knock through the brush. Compared to the Coho, our trip upstream is efficient. After a lifetime in the ocean, they swim all the way back to the stream they were born in. I think about those nature shows with the bear in the river, gorging on fish that practically leap into his paws as they battle the current. Life's a bitch. Lara says the hatcheries have a much higher success rate than the fish who fend for themselves. She talks percentages as Lucky grips the tailgate with one hand, smokes with the other.

"This your job?" she asks me.

"Volunteer."

"I used to work downtown," she offers. "They call me Lucky 'cause I got busted around the time all my girlfriends went to the pig farm." Throws her head back and cackles. She's referring to a local farmer who was convicted of killing six women. Newspapers with photographs of missing women from the Downtown Eastside set the number closer to fifty.

"That is lucky," I say, wondering what's so funny.

She looks me over: black hair, pale skin. "You're not an Indian."

"Métis."

"Half-bloods," she snorts. "You guys are the real nobodies."

I shrug—I'm not getting into this with a *violent offender*. Lara frowns. The truck slips through skunk-cabbage bogs, dark soil seasoned with pine needles. We duck to avoid the slap of low-hanging branches.

It's all wild rose and blackberry at the site, but no blooms this time of year. The last berries scavenged by bears. It doesn't look like the day is going to overcome its fishbowl start; there's a film over everything. The yellow rain gear Diane passes out is a relief. She points to the river—a couple of the Mossom Creek guys are already stringing barrier nets at either end.

"This is Station 1. If you want to work in the river, put on the hip waders," Diane says. "Station 2"—she puts a bucket and some plastic bags on the picnic table—"eggs and milt."

A volunteer emerges from the bushes with a decapitated Coho. He pulls out a knife and sits at the table. One slit, and carnelian-coloured eggs spill out of her belly.

"Sushi," Lucky says and elbows me. "No, really, that's brain food right there." I move to the other side of the table, next to Lara.

"It's true," Diane says, "want some?"

"Nah, my brain's already wasted." Lucky laughs again. Everything's a big joke. She points to the fish bonkers Diane's unloaded from the truck. "I'll kill 'em."

"Station 3, eh?" Diane glances at the guard, who shrugs.

Lucky sees this. "Come on, better the clubs than the knives, right?"

"It's no problem, Lucky," Diane says. "Lara?"

"Where do you want to be?" Lara asks me.

"As far away from Lucky as possible," I say, quiet. She nods. We pull on the hip waders.

"All right, Fishing Bear, show 'em how it's done," Lucky calls.

Diane, unsurprisingly, looks horrified. Half of me is horrified too, the other half kinda wants to laugh.

A few steps in and the river is pushing me around, a downstream shove over polished rocks. Now I'm in the way of progress. Around me, the Coho are boiling. Their panic is tangible but so is their resolve. Green ghosts shoot forward to snap at my calves, then scoot away. Encased in rubber, I still shrink from the contact.

A net proves useless; it bends and pulls when I dip into the current. I slip a little and swear under my breath. Sweat collects along my backbone.

"How do you do this?" I call to Lara, but she's too far away and the river drowns me out. Shouldn't have had that coffee; my heart is pounding. Tweaked. A feeling I've been trying to avoid. My legs stiffen and the force of the river increases, so I bend my knees. This can't be as bad as handling a hive full of bees for the first time, when they seem terrifying, before you realize that you're the Godzilla. I look down. The water is full of fish and all I have to do is reach in and grab one. Inhale, plunge a hand into the river, and connect five fingers with a solid body. It fights and escapes. I swing the net around, tie it onto my back, and try again, with both hands this time. I've never seen Coho teeth, not sure how much damage they'd do. Lara watches for a sec, then she ditches her net and gets in there next to me.

Got one this time, right at the base of the tail. Heave and he's in my arms. I was not expecting this: hook-faced, black-lipped, red-bellied sea monster. One eye missing, ripped fins, torn skin. He's winding me—fights with more strength than seems possible from a body already half decomposed.

I hang on, restraining a Mossom Creek Coho at the unforeseen end to his homecoming. Whispering hollow assurance: Lara's percentages, chances of increased fry survival. Don't be afraid. Do not fear that woman on the shore, your executioner. You won't meet death in your own river, what you were hoping for, I admit. But your DNA will be preserved, and that's what it's all about, really.

I don't know if he hears me. He stops fighting. Diane and

the others are waiting on the shore with clubs and knives. Salmon enhancement. Nature's Little Calipers. I think about the bees at the end of their *productive life cycle*, but there's no time to think, really, before the river shoves me back toward Lucky. "C'mon, Fishing Bear!" She waves the fish bonker over her head and whoops like an Indian in a John Wayne Western. Diane and the crew look at their feet.

"What a comedian," Lara says. But I'm laughing. I'm not sure if it's okay to laugh, but shit, I'm up to my thighs in pissed-off salmon.

"You're good at this," Lucky says when I give her the fish.

"I'll add it to my resumé," I say.

"We'll go fishing when I get out," she says. "Could be five to ten still though, eh?" And again, even though I'm not quite sure it's okay, we share a laugh like a cigarette. Me in the river, her on the shore.

Lara gets the next one, a female. Flushed and grinning, she hands it off to Diane. Now some of the Station 2 volunteers are thinking that this fishing by hand is looking very primal and authentic, so they wade in with us. We pull salmon out of the river for hours. On the shore, humans cut eggs out of bellies, and squirt fish sperm into plastic bags, until it's time for hot drinks and peanut butter sandwiches.

"Don't you find this all a bit weird?" I ask Lucky over a hot chocolate, like we're chatting at Starbucks or something.

"What, the egg take? Like she says, it's better for the fish." Lucky nods her head at Lara, who looks vindicated. "It's still weird though."

After lunch, some of the volunteers gather around Diane. She dissects a Coho for those who have never seen a fish from the inside. Lara and I have both seen a fish from the inside, but we join in anyway. Diane cuts the organs out one by one and piles them in a bloody clump: a purple heart, a liver, a swim bladder. When she cuts into the face, we all cringe a little. She gives Lara an eyeball and Lara balances it on the tip of her finger. Through the lens, Lara and I see the world upside down. River in the sky. Diane's bloody knife. The blackberry canes where Lucky's been hidden, since nobody wants to see the fish meet their end. She's still working away, fish after fish, soft thud against flesh. She says something I can't make out, and laughs. I can't see her, but through the fish eye, I think I see Lucky's upside-down laughter run down to the ground like honey. Absorb near the tree roots.

CHARLIE FISET

IF I EVER SEE THE SUN

And now tell me how he rapt you away to the realm of
darkness and gloom, and by what trick did the strong
Host of Many beguile you?

> —Demeter to Persephone,
> *The Homeric Hymn to Demeter*

A t the end of her shift, Roxane sits down on a wooden
bench under the shack at 1000 level. She waits for the
cage with the rest of the men. Air from the heater
warms the side of her face against the frigid drafts that pour
down from the surface through the shaft. The shack has a
wooden floor, ancient and resinous under a layer of grit; there's
a partition beside her that seems oddly out of place, and behind
her head there's a round bolt in the wood, just below chest
level, with three rusty chain links hanging down from it.

Sixty years ago, the shack housed mules that carted ore
through the drifts. They lived beneath the surface; once they'd
been brought down they never saw the light of day. Maybe

when they became obsolete the mules were hauled up in the cage. Maybe they were brought to a farm with misty valleys where they could live out their retirement eating all the lush, green grass they wanted, the sun warming their greying withers. Or maybe, Roxane thinks, their bones lie quiet, scattered in the dark, dust blending with the broken rock.

The cage whispers down on the wheels like a promise. When it slides into sight and stops at the level, Roxane gets up and grabs her steel lunch kit. Her arm jars, jerking her back down to the bench. She yanks the lunch kit again but it's stuck.

"What's the holdup?" the shift-boss yells from the gate. There's sniggering in the dark cage behind him. "You need some help with that? Too much heavy lifting today?"

When she flips the locks and opens the lid, she sees nothing at first, but then she lifts the paper towel she wraps her apples in and sees two little black holes like tooth punctures in the centre of the greasy steel underneath. The kit's been nailed down to the bench.

Roxane leaves it there and squeezes into the cage, shoulder-to-quaking-shoulder, trying to laugh with everybody else. As they start the ascent she takes a deep breath and lets gravity push her weight deep into the thick soles of her boots, glad nobody can see her face.

"Don't worry," says Gloria, the cage-operator. "They're only joking. They love jokes."

The cage is one of the only places in the mine where it's quiet enough to talk; you can almost hear a whisper over the contented sigh of the conveyance as the cage is guided up the shaft by the line. The cool smooth sound of the wheels and runners against the wooden shaft guides could almost lull you to sleep. But Roxane has to strain to listen to Gloria because of his English. It's unique to the area and possibly to the mine, where a small subgroup of the language—mostly French mixed with universal miner's lingo—had been patched together by the sixty workers that drove in from Quebec.

"You keep the machines in good order," Gloria says. "You don't drive too fast or too slow, you help unload the ANFO. You're a good girl. You keep working hard, keep proving yourself, and one day you'll be the one nailing lunch kits to the bench." He laughs and then coughs, and Roxane can hear the phlegm shift in his throat.

When Roxane first started working underground, Gloria gave her a pair of his old boots and coveralls. It was hard to find the right size because no manufacturer made them small enough for women. Gloria's wife made alterations for him because he was only five-foot-three. Being so small with a name like "Gloria," Roxane thought he'd know something about jokes, but nobody ever laughed at him—not even when he was trying to be funny.

"If they didn't like you," Gloria continues, "they'd laugh a different way."

"Like they laugh at Wycliffe Nichols?" Roxane asks, trying not to sound angry.

Last shift, Wycliffe was driving the locomotive and its floor fell out from underneath him. The locis are made collapsible so they can be folded up and put into the cage, moved to the tracks on different levels. When the loci's floor collapsed, Wycliffe had to run on the tracks in the gap between the frame until he could get the loci stopped. If Wycliffe had stopped running or fallen he would've been cut in half. The men laughed at the sight of him running for his life. The shift-boss just stood there, laughing with the rest of them. Roxane hadn't known what to do.

Gloria says, "You can't blame them. Wycliffe deserves what he gets."

Roxane knows he means what he says because she can see his face lit up at intervals when the cage passes the golden lights at each level, shining through the gates. Before she can ask what he means, he calls: "Now listen up, everybody. I'm not supposed to tell you, but the second we get to the surface the Captain's going through everybody's lunch kits."

"Why?" someone asks.

"Things have been going missing around here. Management thinks the miners might be stealing stuff. I'm sure none of you has anything to worry about." He elbows Roxane and says to her loudly, "especially you, because you forgot your lunch kit."

In the seconds after Gloria falls silent there's a nervous shuffling of heavy boots. Then a *clang* of something heavy hitting the cage floor. Another *clang*, *clang* . . . *clang*. Roxane jumps when something sharp and hard *thunks* her steel-toe.

The cage doors open suddenly, almost unexpectedly; light floods the cage. It's always a nice feeling, Roxane thinks, when the cage hits the collar and you see sun through the windows. But today she worked the nightshift and the sun won't be up before she finishes her drive home.

The men pile out quicker than usual, leaving just Gloria and Roxane standing there, blinking. The floor is littered with wrenches and ratchet heads and a portable safety line—there's even a roll of toilet paper, a muddy boot tread mashing up the tissue.

"What the hell . . . ?" Roxane mutters.

Gloria's laughing so hard he can barely say "There was no check! The stupid asses!"

⸎

Roxane hates driving the loci alone on 4000 level because it's where the fire started. It had been more than twenty years, but there were miners still working who remembered the two dead men's faces, what they were like at The Miner's Inn on Friday nights. There's a plaque on the drift with the names and the date of the fire. The plaque always glints in Roxane's headlamp when she drives the loci past, winking at her in the dark. Gloria told her a fire's the worst thing that can happen in a mine. The smoke has nowhere to go when the power's out and the fans aren't working. This whole place breathes through a tiny little hole in the surface, he said, just like how you breathe out of tiny holes in your face. If the hole gets clogged, the whole body dies. There was nothing left of those two boys but their shadows on the rock.

"What do you mean?" she had asked.

"Branded into the rock," he'd said again, "like at Hiroshima."

She still didn't understand, but didn't want to ask him again because he might have thought she didn't believe him— or worse, that she was afraid.

When she drives the loci by an intersection at a subdrift, the loci's headlight shines down and carves the tunnel as deep as the light goes, but no farther. The darkness collapses behind her. Usually there's always buzzing in the mine, the hissing of pneumatics and the hard tinny vibration of diesel engines rebounding off the walls, filling up the dark with sound. But the loci's battery-powered and quiet except for the sound of the gliding wheels on the rails.

Roxane sees a light up ahead, down the drift. It's faint but too big to be a headlamp. She blows the horn. The light doesn't move. She tries the horn again. She can't stand the way the sound expands and fleshes out the drift, turning it into the ribbed gut of a bloated worm.

Before she can break, the loci starts slowing on its own. Something underneath her feet feels different, the pull of the wheels gone slack. Then the loci's headlights go out. The loci glides to a complete stop and Roxane's left staring down the drift at the light in the distance—she's sure they're headlights now, a Kubota, probably.

Son of a bitch. Roxane switches on her headlamp and turns off the loci's motor in case the battery kicks in again while she's out looking for the Femco phone so she can call a mechanic. It's the third time this month that the battery's died on her. The last time she had to spend five hours waiting in the dark. When it happened to the other guys they just stretched back in the driver's seat and slept like the dead, but Roxane had never been able to sleep underground.

She jumps down onto the track, water spattering from her boots, and starts toward the light in the distance. The Kubota is empty but still running. Farther down the drift she sees the steel rails of a grizzly sitting overtop a dark patch on the ground that her headlamp won't light up—it's the chute where trainloads of ore are dumped. The grizzly stops all the really big muck from going down the hole and plugging the chute below. A fifteen-pound sledge is sitting near the hole. Somebody must have been working on the grizzly with the hammer to break up the big muck so it could fall down the chute.

"Hello?" she calls. "Hello?"

Nobody answers.

Whoever's been working on the grizzly must still be there because of the Kubota. *Maybe he's broken down too*, she thinks. *Maybe I'll meet whoever it is on my way to the Femco.* As she starts to walk on, she sees a glint of blue-silver reflecting on the bottom of the drift. A safety lanyard, lying in a puddle that mirrors her shady self back up at her when her lamp light glints off its surface. *But why wouldn't he drive the Kubota to the Femco?* she wonders.

Roxane sweeps her lamplight across the ground, checking to see if someone's fallen; then she squats down and checks under the Kubota. But there's nobody. She follows the lanyard, walking slow at first, then quicker. The line cuts off suddenly, disappearing into darkness underneath the grizzly. It's hanging down into the chute.

The chute is dark and still and quiet but she can feel, or she imagines she feels, stirring in the air. She climbs up onto the grizzly and shines her light down.

There's a body dangling ten feet below. It's attached to the lanyard, twisting slightly against the chute like a fly on a spider's strand. Otherwise, unmoving.

"Shit," Roxane says, "shit shit *shit*."

It's Wycliffe Nichols. His head is lolling downward, lipless mouth hanging open under his wide, blunt nose. He looks dead.

"Shit," Roxane says again. Wycliffe jerks.

Roxane leaps back, boot tread catching on the rail so she feels the darkness below her teeter and then ascend, reaching up to grab her like a widespread palm.

Wycliffe's voice sounds up through the chute like he's yelling from the bottom of a well, so loud in the quiet.

"Help me! God, help me. Jesus, help me!"

"It's okay," Roxane calls, trying for a steady voice. "It's going to be okay."

"Jesus, help me. Jesus, help me."

He's looking up at her, eyes wide with naked fear.

"I don't have a radio," she calls. "I'll go find a Femco. I'll be right back—"

"Don't leave! I can't get down. You need to cut me down."

It's a hundred feet down to the next level. If Roxane cuts him down, he'll fall to his death. There's something funny about the way he's talking, and his eyes are too big and too black. He might be concussed. He might be in shock. His back might be broken. That's why he's jerking like a worm on a hook in the gaping maw of the chute.

"I'll get help—"

"He's coming back!" Wycliffe says, his voice taking on a different kind of panic. "Don't leave me. Dear God, don't leave me alone down here with him!"

"What are you talking about?"

"He did this to me. It was *him*."

As far as Roxane could tell nobody had done anything to Wycliffe. It looked like he was working the fifteen-pound sledge on top of the grizzly and he forgot to unclip his safety lanyard before driving away in the Kubota. When he ran out of line he got pulled out of the Kubota and down the drift and then he fell down the chute. He should be dead.

"He's there!" Wycliffe says again. "Behind you!"

Roxane resists the urge to whirl around; she knows nobody's

out on the rail with her. But even as she thinks it, a whisper of wind stirs the loose strands of hair that have fallen from her braid, prickling the hairs on the nape of her neck.

She digs in the pocket of her coveralls and finds her spare light, sets the flashlight on the grizzly rail so it shines over the top of the chute. "Don't worry," she says. "I'll be back in one minute."

"Don't you leave me, you bitch!" Wycliffe screams. "Don't leave me alone in the dark with him—"

His shouts chase Roxane down the drift, headlamp arcing back and forth as she stumbles on the jagged, slippery rock. There are Femco phones every half-kilometre. She jumps into the Kubota so she can drive down the drift but then remembers the loci's blocking the way. Her breaths rattle in her ears as she runs. She passes the Femco the first time, backtracks and finds it, makes the call.

⦿⦿⦿

She finds out a few days later that Wycliffe has some broken ribs but is otherwise fine. "He's damn lucky," Gloria says. "He's always been damn lucky."

Roxane tells Gloria that when the Mine Rescue team had Wycliffe strapped to the stretcher Wycliffe was raving. "He said, 'I can feel it in the rock! Can't you feel it? Can't you? It's the quiet before the big burst.'" Roxane hesitates. "He said we're all going to burn."

"That crazy bastard," Gloria says. "He was in shock. He didn't know what he was saying. And he's a nutcase, anyway. He didn't like being on that stretcher, probably. You know what happened the last time they had him on a stretcher? He had volunteered to play the injured man when the Mine Rescuers were practising for a competition. He was strapped down, and they were administering oxygen to him through a facemask attached to a hose. When they were finishing up the exercise, the Captain detached the hose and farted in it. Everybody thought it was so funny that they passed the hose around until everyone on the team had a turn farting." Gloria laughs so hard he hacks up a wad of phlegm and spits it, *plop*, on the floor of the cage. Roxane's glad he can't see her making a face.

"When they were carrying him away, he said there was somebody down there," she says. "Somebody who whispers in your ear in the dark."

Gloria laughs. "Yeah, that sounds like Wycliffe," he mutters.

"*I* felt somebody standing behind me," Roxane says. "It sounds crazy, but I did."

"I've felt and seen and heard all kinds of strange things down here," Gloria says. "But I can explain all of them. Underground is the darkest dark there is—it plays funny tricks on your imagination, especially if you're half-crazy already. You can put whatever's in your head into that dark space in front of your eyes. And once it's there it never goes away again." Gloria laughs. "No, I wouldn't put too much stock in what old Wycliffe Nichols says."

"Why not?"

"Wycliffe should have died in the fire along with the two Mine Rescue men, but somehow he survived. And nobody's ever forgiven him. Maybe because he says Jesus saved him."

"What's wrong with that?"

"He meant it was Jesus who pulled him up to the refuge station when he was passed out."

"Oh," says Roxane.

"When they found Wycliffe and Wycliffe told them what happened, the Captain had to take his bullshit story seriously. They thought maybe one of the other miners had saved him, someone who hadn't signed out before leaving. So they sent more Mine Rescue men down to the lower levels to see if someone was trapped, and that's when those two boys got trapped themselves. Maybe he's not crazy," says Gloria. "But Jesus has a sick sense of justice if he kept Wycliffe around and let the other two burn. You can't have scum like that working underground."

The cage hits the collar, the door opens, and everybody files out into the amber light like fool's gold that floods the drift near the refuge station.

Roxane is working down on 4000 level again. But this time she's not alone. On the way back and forth to the chute she can hear voices every time she passes one of the sublevels.

When she parks the loci and walks down the drift, she sees that the sublevel's filled with people: geologists and the shift-boss, and a bunch of miners. Their shadows dance tall and monstrous on the drift wall behind them as they titter excitedly, huddling together, walking back and forth and pointing. They've been drilling with longhole machines and blasting to get at the ore-filled stope. The subdrift's a mess of broken muck and puddles of water. A silent, squat scoop sits in front of the stope, covered in dust like a calcified, caged animal long forgotten.

"What's going on?" Roxane asks.

It looks like there's something written on the drift wall. The marks are like pressed leaves, stippled dots in striped ridges forming vaguely round shapes.

"They're fossils," one of the geologists says. "They're over 4.6 billion years old. Those things used to be all over the Earth."

"Too bad we have to blow 'em up," says one of the miners. He's taking pictures with his phone, the flash wiping out the darkness in between the hole-punches of the headlamps. "Look at 'em. Aren't they evil-looking little buggers? They're just like a big grub or a centipede. I hate the sight of them. Why do you suppose that is? Why do you think I hate the sight of them so much?"

<hr/>

After Roxane's delivered her last load, she parks the loci and hooks up the battery so she can charge it for the next shift. But it's still forty minutes until the cage comes so she walks down the ramp to the subdrift where they found the fossils. Everybody's gone, probably waiting for the cage, but the fossils are still grinning down at her.

They are ugly, she thinks. They writhe this way and that when she turns her head and drags the light across the rock to look at each of them in turn. Their depths well up with shadow, making them look real, like they'd been trapped alive for millions of years, just waiting to stretch out their ventricular legs and crawl away.

Roxane's light dips down to the big chunks of muck lying in front of the stope. The same stippled dots and cracked-open shells lie in broken heaps on the ground around her feet. A long, cucumber-shaped imprint with ridges down its middle leaps into shadowy movement, gnawing at her steel-toe.

She takes a slow step backward and turns around. There's a light in the distance, a headlamp. She feels a jolt when she realizes somebody's been standing there, watching her.

The headlamp arcs from side to side, and then shines around in a circle; he's rolling his head. It's the sign for "to me." "Come closer," he's saying. She starts to walk toward him, feet crunching fossil dust.

"Hello?" Roxane calls.

The miner makes no reply except to keep swinging his head, saying "closer" again and again.

"What is it?" Roxane yells. "Is something wrong?"

No answer.

When she gets to within ten feet of him she stops. He's standing in the centre of the subdrift, blocking the way to the main drift where the loci's parked.

"Who are you?" Roxane asks. She can see the shadows of his legs in the penumbra of her headlamp, thinner and longer than they should be. She's been walking forward with her head bowed to avoid shining her light in the man's eyes. But she can't stand the dark silence stretching between them, so she lifts her light, trying to get a look at him.

Before she can see his face, the man steps into the shadows and she loses sight of him.

Roxane's breath catches in her throat. There's a sudden *crack* and a jarring feeling in her neck and then she's in the dark. She realizes that the bastard broke her headlamp with something heavy, a wrench or a hammer.

"What the fuck?" she tries to say, but the words won't come. She takes a step back, reaches into her coveralls for the flashlight she always carries. But she pulls it out too quick and drops it. It clanks down onto the drift, and Roxane knows it could be a foot away and she won't find it in the dark, even if she crawls on her hands and knees looking.

Think. Don't panic. What are you supposed to do when your lamp goes out? Sit down in the dark and wait for somebody to come find you. You wouldn't get more than twenty feet walking blind in a goldmine—you'd fall, maybe down an open chute.

But then she feels hot breath on her face, rank as sulphur.

She takes a step backward, then another. Then another, and then she's running through the dark. Once she gets out onto the drift there'll be the light of the loci in the distance and she could run through the black without tripping too much, using the light to guide her blind feet. She thinks she can hear heavy boots thudding along behind her in the dark. The sound is getting closer, almost in time with her own footfalls. Then she's falling, and for a moment that stretches too long she loses all sense of up and down.

She hits the ground hard, relief bursting forth with the air from her lungs. The drift is on an incline underneath her and she knows she's on the ramp that leads up out of the subdrift.

Get up. But now that she's down she feels like she could stay still and wait for help; whoever's on the subdrift with her is as blind as she is. She could disappear into the dark. Eventually somebody would find her. But she knows if she stays and waits she'll never come back underground again. *Get up*, she thinks. *Get up. Just get up.*

When she crests the ramp and rounds the corner out of the subdrift the warm circle of the loci's lights glows in the near-distance, showering gradients of penumbra closer and closer until her feet break the light and she is no longer as dark as the darkness; she can see a part of herself again. When she reaches the loci she sits down in the driver's seat and turns it on and starts to drive before she even tries to catch her breath.

"Don't read too much into it," says Gloria when he's taking her up to the surface. "It was a nasty joke. Just somebody messing with you. One of the old-timers giving you a hard time. It'll teach you to never shine your light in someone's eyes, anyway."

<hr/>

Roxane's next shift's cancelled because a slow trickle of water built up somewhere above 1000 level and then blasted out of a ten-by-ten chute holding five hundred tonnes of muck. Someone was taking muck out of the raise at the bottom with a scoop, and when they'd taken enough the water gave way all at once, burying a brand new scoop in rubble after moving it two hundred feet down the drift. It could have killed some-body. As it was, the scoop operator who got hit was in the hospital with a collapsed lung and a broken wrist. Roxane real-izes, only after she sees the muck blown down the drift, that she was tramming near the chute on the day the water gave. If the man in the dark hadn't broken her light she might have been the one laid up in the hospital, or worse.

"Maybe that's what Wycliffe was talking about," Roxane says to Gloria. She's trying to sound like she doesn't believe.

"In a place like this it's a miracle accidents don't happen more often," Gloria says. "And if they keep happening, they're going to close this place down. They won't shut us down just because people keep getting hurt. They'll close when the bad morale causes production to get so low there'll be no point in keeping it open anymore."

Roxane knows what'll happen if they close the mine. She remembers growing up playing on streets lined with derelict houses and broken fences hemming in overgrown lawns. The downtown strip was burned down and boarded up. Everything slept quietly, lying nascent until another company came in wanting to refine the old tailings or strike down to another mother lode.

"They dug too deep," Gloria says. "And they didn't fill in the ground properly. It's dangerous here. Why does a nice, pretty girl like you want to work in a hole like this, anyway?"

"I need money," Roxane says.

"You can get money working on top of the ground."

"I can't make enough money working anywhere else. I have a little girl, and she's got nobody but me."

"What about her daddy?"

"He was one of the boys who went missing in the forest fire a few years back," Roxane says.

On the news they said that the fire front changed direction in the wind at the last minute, trapping the crews that were working at the front. They had to resort to their emergency survival plan: digging a big trench in the ground, as deep as they could get it before the flames and smoke got too close, and then pulling a big fireproof tarp over their heads in the hope that the fire would burn over them. But they were never found.

"I'm sorry," says Gloria. "I am sorry to hear that. But your little girl's the reason to get out. You're not planning on staying down here forever, are you?"

"What about Wycliffe?" Roxane asks, trying to change the subject. "He looks like he's seventy, anyway."

"He was retired until just a few years ago. It's funny you should mention the fire. Wycliffe had a hobby farm, and he lost everything in the fire—his whole property went up. He had to start working again. But he's done now, after that with the Kubota. Good riddance, I say. He's too old to work anymore. He's dangerous. Crazy."

⚬⚬⚬

At the end of her next shift, just after Roxane has parked the loci and she's walking back to the cage, she sees the solitary headlamp again. The light starts to roll in the dark—"come closer."

This time she stays where she is. "Who are you?" she calls. "What the hell do you want?"

The light stops rolling and starts to bob gently up and down. He's walking toward her.

"Stop!" Roxane shouts. "Stop right there!" She shines her lamp at the man's head.

"Will you get that fucking light out of my eyes?" the shift-boss says.

"Sorry."

"Listen, I think there's a power outage. The phones are down, and I can't get ahold of anybody. I want you to go to the refuge station and wait there till I come back. If you meet anybody on the way, tell them the same thing."

"What's happening?" Roxane asks. "Is something wrong?"

"It's nothing," he says. "Don't worry about it."

His frame jitters in the light while he walks away. No jokes now. He hurries over the uneven ground, splashing through the puddles without seeing them.

When Roxane gets to the refuge she finds it empty. The lights don't work, but she still has her headlamp. She closes the big steel door behind her. It's set in a concrete wall, designed to block the refuge off from the rest of the mine. The refuge floor is concrete too, but the other walls are jagged, bare rock. She picks up the phone that's mounted beside safety procedure posters on a piece of plywood backing. But the line is dead.

She sits down on one of the picnic tables in the middle of the room, the dark air pressing down on her shoulders. Maybe it's just a power outage. Or maybe there's something wrong with the cage. It happened three or four times a year that the hoist got tangled or something went wrong with the winch. The last time a shift got stuck underground, they had to wait for hours. The Captain was thinking about making them climb up to the surface in the escapeway.

Roxane feels the air stir, a herald of movement unseen. She holds her breath. There it is. The steady wheeze of slow, deep breathing.

Slowly, she shines her light around the circumference of the room, starting in the corner nearest to her. Her light catches in the crags, playing tricks on her eyes. She's almost swept the entire room; still, there's nothing. But in the last corner her light slides over a bundle of rags, slides back. Roxane leaps to her feet.

A pair of eyes blink open, glassy and reflective in the light. It's Wycliffe Nichols.

"Why the hell didn't you say anything when I walked in?" Roxane asks.

"I didn't know who you were," Wycliffe says. "I couldn't see your face. You might have been *him*."

He's curled up in a dozen pairs of old, dirty coveralls, Roxane realizes.

"What's going on out there?" he asks. "Why's the power down?"

"Shift-boss sent me to the refuge," Roxane says. "He says he's going to find a radio. The phones are down. He's coming back soon."

"He won't be back," Wycliffe says. "No, we've seen the last of old Roger. Old Roger who likes a good joke."

"What's that supposed to mean?"

Wycliffe's voice is hoarse, as if he hasn't spoken for days. His breaths rattle around a moist cough that sounds like it issues from infected lungs. Though he's sleeping in a nest of them, he's not wearing any coveralls—just dirty jeans and a flannel shirt. His boots are tall, insulated rubber ones like the kind Roxane's father used to wear to shovel the driveway. He has no hardhat.

"Where's all your gear?" Roxane asks. Wycliffe makes no answer.

"I thought you were out with broken ribs? Gloria said you weren't coming back. I didn't see you in the cage today."

"I didn't come down in the cage," Wycliffe says. "I know how to get in from the surface. I climbed down, a few days ago."

"You've been *living* down here? But why would you come back?" she asks. Then it hits her. "It was you who broke my light, wasn't it? You've been creeping around in the dark—"

"Break your light? What are you talking about? I didn't break no light. It was *him* who broke your light."

"You're a crazy bastard."

"You've seen him too, haven't you?" says Wycliffe. "That day you found me hanging in the chute you felt him. I could ask you who he is, as much as you could ask me. Does he ever come up on you so you can only see his legs in the shadows outside your headlamp? Does your light chase him away when you try to get closer? His breath smells like sulphur, doesn't it?"

"You're crazy," she says again. She heads for the refuge door.

"I wouldn't go out there if I were you," Wycliffe says. "He says there's trouble."

Roxane pauses.

"I know why he's after me," Wycliffe says. "I know what sleeps on my conscience. But why's he after *you*? There's only one reason he finds you in the dark."

"What do you mean?" Roxane asks.

"He's not bad. You might think he is, but he's only trying to help you."

Roxane remembered how the drift had flooded and crushed the scoop, how she'd been saved.

"You said he pushed you down the chute," Roxane says.

"I didn't say that. I said it was his fault, and it was. He told me to jump from the Kubota at the last second. Otherwise, my spine would have snapped like a twig. He wasn't trying to hurt me. He was telling me how to survive."

"Is that what *he* told you the day those two boys got killed in the fire?" Roxane asks.

Wycliffe's silent for a long time. Then he says, "He tells me lots of things. He tells me when the rock's about to burst. He tells me when they're laying charges and one doesn't go off. He's been keeping me alive for a long, long time."

Roxane remembers what Gloria told her, about Wycliffe saying he was saved by Jesus. "He's been keeping *you* alive," she laughs. But she doesn't like the way her voice sounds hollow and scared in the darkness, so she asks, "Why?"

"I don't know. There's no rhyme or reason for it. He told me about today. That's why he let me get in that Kubota with my lanyard still on. He wanted me to be far away from this place, safe in the hospital. But I came back. I'm not going to let him help me no more."

"What do you mean?" Roxane asks.

"Today's the day," Wycliffe says. "I don't know if it's a cave-in or a rock burst. Or maybe it's another fire. But it's coming. And it's going to happen soon. From the looks of things, it's happening already."

"Stop talking shit," Roxane says.

"I've had a good life," he says. "God knows I didn't deserve what happiness I got. I had a little place on the water where the thrushes sang in the morning and the mallards came to nest in the spring and swam in between the shore and the ice on the lake. And every night in summer the loons called out over the water. When the sun set after real hot days and the gulls flew through the mist the barges would float by, playing music. And there'd be the sound of people laughing. I'd give anything to get just a taste of that place one more time. I'd give anything—"

"I said shut up," says Roxane.

The darkness stretches between them, hardens, and grows cold. She wants to leave the refuge; she wills herself to get up again, open the door, but it's only a dream. She's sitting still.

"Maybe I'm wrong," Wycliffe says. "Maybe it's all right this time."

"Gloria says you should have died in that fire twenty years ago," Roxane says. She's keeping her eyes and her light on him, as if worried he'll suddenly spring at her, or slither off into the darkness.

"I should have," Wycliffe says. "But I didn't."

"So what did you do? How did you *really* survive?"

She expects him to tell her the same crock of shit he's been spouting for twenty years, but instead he says, "You ever smell the stench?"

"Stench?"

"I was down on 4000 when I smelled it. They make it smell that way, so you can't confuse it with the taste of second-hand air, or anything else. It wrenches your gut. They flood the mine with it when there's an emergency. If you smell that smell something's gone wrong. The first thing you're supposed to do is get to a Femco, tell someone where you are. But when I got to the phone the lines were down, and that's how I knew the power was out. So I headed for the refuge. I couldn't see or hear anything out of the ordinary, except that it was too quiet. But I wasn't in any special hurry as I made my way down to the refuge station. It wasn't until I came out of the subdrift that I started to see smoke. Soon I couldn't see my hand in front of my face. My headlamp didn't help. It just shone on the smoke and threw the light back in my eyes. I didn't know how far away the refuge was. And the smoke was getting thicker. It was getting difficult to breathe. It didn't take me too long to realize that there was a fire burning somewhere in front of me. I got all turned around. I didn't know which way I'd come from. The smoke was so thick that I knew it'd be a matter of minutes before I lost consciousness . . . But I could see the smoke eddying a few feet in front of me. I realized I must be close to a ventilation raise. So I kept on, feeling my way along the drift until I came to the raise. And I stood there, breathing in the fresh air from the surface. I was stuck at the raise but the air kept me alive."

"That really works?" Roxane asks.

"Of course it does. But the ventilation raises are also what they use to spread the stench around the mine. So when you're squatting under there, praying to God that someone will find you, you're breathing in each breath of the worst smell you've ever smelled in your life, and you're thinking all the while that each breath is sweet because it could be your last."

"How long were you there for?"

"I don't know. Time passed differently. If nobody had come for me by now, I thought, it probably meant that the fire was bad, and getting worse. Other people must be trapped. I was the only one on 4000. Knowing this didn't make the time go any faster. I knew I needed to get to a refuge. Once you're in there, you can clay up the door and wait—you can last for days. When I first found the vent I didn't know where I was, but as I stood there things started to become clear. I was almost sure I knew which way to go. But picking the wrong way would kill me. I guess I was waiting for a sign."

"A sign?" Roxane asks.

"Something to let me know, beyond a doubt, that it would be better to try to find the refuge than to stay under the ventilation shaft. And I did see a sign."

"What did you see?"

"A flash of light through the smoke. Just a flicker. It might not have been anything at all. I thought maybe it was somebody from Mine Rescue, looking for men on the drifts. I called out, but there was no answer."

"Then what?" Roxane asks.

"I blacked out," Wycliffe says. "Maybe I inhaled too much smoke. Or maybe I had some kind of panic attack. I woke up in the dark and I thought I was dead. My light was off. But it didn't take too long to figure out I was in a refuge. And I could *feel* that I wasn't alone in the dark. I heard the sound of a door opening—the refuge station door, I knew that sound. 'Hello?' I called, but my voice was torn up by the smoke. Nobody answered. I tried to turn on my headlamp, but the bulb was smashed. I remembered I had a flashlight in my pocket. I was so nervous when I pulled it out that I almost dropped it. 'Wait!' I called. 'Wait!' I wanted to see the face of the man who'd saved my life. I got my light out just in time. I saw him."

"Who did you see?" Roxane asks, even though she knows what Wycliffe's answer will be.

"His face was long and thin and white. He had a big, round, black hole for a mouth. And his eyes . . . I'll never forget his eyes. They were more like teeth than they were like eyes. Sharp and white. They ate me up. Then spat out the bones, and now the bones are all that's left." Wycliffe's face is stretched in agony. "It was the *Beast*," he whispers. "It was the Devil who saved my life. And it's been him following me around in the dark all these years."

Roxane swallows. "I thought . . . I thought you said you saw Jesus."

The smell hits both of them at the same time. It's gut-wrenching, breathing in the first lungful, just like Wycliffe said. It's so thick Roxane thinks it'll crowd out all the oxygen in her lungs, fill up her blood.

"What is that?" she asks, but she already knows.

"Stay here, and I'll be all right," Wycliffe mutters. "Stay right here. Clay the door, sit tight, and wait for someone to come get me. I'll be all right if I wait . . ."

He rises to his feet and heads for the refuge station door, kicking the tangle of coveralls away from him. He opens one of the lockers and pulls out the emergency supplies and lays them on the ground near the door.

"You make sure you use this," he says.

"What?"

"Clay the door, and then crack an air header on the two-inch pipe. That'll fix the pressure so no smoke can get in."

"What do you mean?" Roxane asks. "You're not going out there—"

Wycliffe heaves the door open. The curling tendrils of smoke pause upon the threshold, then pull him out the door and into the drift, so white with smoke she can't see the rock on the other side. He hauls the door shut behind him.

Roxane's headlamp reflects off the steel, showing her a ghostly shape—a long, white face with shaded eyes. She starts, looking behind her. But no one's there. It's her own reflection staring back at her.

The crazy bastard, she thinks. *He won't get a hundred metres. I'm not getting myself killed going after his sorry corpse—*

An image of Johnny flashes into her thoughts. Twenty men died huddled under that tarp, waiting in the dark for the flames to burn overtop of them.

If you sit tight you'll be all right. That's what Wycliffe said. *Someone will come for you.*

Roxane drops back down to the picnic table. Minutes pass. The rock walls writhe. She hears something; her light sweeps the room, finally focusing on a shape, matte shadow in the moist grey-black, a shape that shouldn't be there. It's another fossil, small and jagged and curved upward like a smile, jabbering through clenched teeth. The word *"escapeway"* dissipates in the air like a whisper. Roxane can't tell if she heard it in the darkness in front of her eyes or the darkness inside her head.

She climbs to her feet and opens the locker near the door, digs through until she finds a breather—a "self-rescuer," they're called. They can last up to one hour.

If she could only get to the escapeway . . . It's four thousand rungs to the top. She had to climb it once, back when she was in training. There was a bum-ledge every twenty metres, where you could sit and rest. When you got to within five hundred metres of the surface you started to see the top of the tunnel, just a tiny prick of light. All you had to do was keep pulling it closer. That wouldn't be the hard part, anyway; the hard part would be finding the escapeway in the smoke.

When she opens the door smoke billows into the refuge. The two hundred metres to the ladder might as well be two kilometres. If she misses it and has to double back . . .

No. Don't think about that. The escapeway would be safe because they send air down the raise from the surface. And the fire will be downwind of the escapeway, if it's on 4000 at all.

She keeps her hand on the side of the drift, measuring each step at a metre, counting her steps to keep track of the distance. Two hundred steps, then four thousand rungs. Then she can breathe the clean, free air and see the daylight.

As she walks through the white, the smoke clawing at her eyes, she thinks of Johnny again.

There were no fires in the north that year, so Johnny and his crew were being shipped off to California to help put out the wildfires that were burning up the state. He ended up having to stay at the last minute because of the fire that broke out and ate up half the town.

Roxane's hand slides into nothing and she knows she's found the entrance to the escapeway. She gropes for the first rung, latches on, pulls herself up. Starts the long climb.

Just past 4000 level, she hears footfalls sounding on the rungs below her, a split-second after her own.

"Wycliffe?" she calls, but the sound's thrown back in her mouth by the breather mask she forgot to take off. She pulls the mask down and takes a slow, deep lungful of air, fresh and sweet like it'll be on the surface. There's a landing in front of her and she wants to stop and rest and breathe deep, free lungfuls—but she doesn't dare. She keeps pulling herself up and up and up, arms burning, chest heaving.

A pinprick of light blinks into existence above her head, like the first star in the night sky. She makes a wish, chances a look down. Sees only darkness. Maybe she imagined the footfalls, after all. Maybe she only dreamed the heavy breathing, the broken headlamp, the long, shadowy legs rooted just outside the circle of her light. She keeps climbing.

Soon she can see her hands on the rungs, her knuckles white when they close around the cold steel. She can almost feel the rosy warm touch of the sun on her cheeks. She tells herself, *The burning in your arms and legs is nothing to what you'd feel if you were burning up in the fire. Nothing like what Johnny felt.*

When she finally reaches the top she stands, hollow and heaving, on the ledge beneath the Plexiglas and wire grating of the trap door that covers the escapeway. Through the glass she can see the rafters of the building that houses the escapeway. Her hands find the trap door's latch. She pushes up.

Nothing happens.

Roxane tries again, heaving with her shoulder. The trap door is stuck. She knows something must be wrong—the escapeway is always open. She pulls a flashlight out of her pocket and shines it through the Plexiglas, shimmying along the ledge, twisting the beam this way and that to try to see what's blocking the trap door. The light refracts strangely around the trap door's edges, turning thick and sluggish like the Plexiglas is coated with lacquer.

"It's ice," Roxane realizes. Frozen shut. Maybe a water main broke; maybe there was a leak in the roof. The mechanics were supposed to check the escapeways but so many things had been going wrong in the mine lately that they must have forgotten.

She'd have to wait.

Eventually, when they couldn't find her underground, the Mine Rescue teams would search. They'd check everywhere. Nobody disappears in a goldmine.

Except the shadowy man, Roxane thinks. Did she hear the scrape of a boot on the rungs of the ladder, just outside of the light that arcs down from the trap door? She looks down into the darkness. Wonders if someone is staring up at her.

"Wycliffe?" she calls.

There's no one, she tells herself. *Wycliffe is dead.*

She could climb back down the ladder, use the breather to get back to the refuge. But the fire might be worse; she might get lost in the smoke. She knows now that she should have stayed, clayed up the door like Wycliffe said. But she couldn't stand the thought of being trapped inside the rock while the world outside was burning. It's better to be trapped by ice than by rock, she thinks—at least there's light.

But it isn't sunlight. The golden fluorescence shining down through the Plexiglas turns the skin of her hands sickly yellow, making her feel like an insect suspended in amber. She remembers what Gloria said: *You can put whatever's in your head into that dark space in front of your eyes. And once it's there it never goes away again.*

Is it Johnny on the ladder? Roxane wonders. Is he the one who's been stalking her in the dark?

A boot scrapes on the rungs again. And now she can hear the deep, wheezing breaths of someone just below her, just out of sight.

"Johnny?" she whispers.

It was only a few days after her seventeenth birthday that she found out she was pregnant with Johnny's child. They'd only had one night together. And now he was leaving for California; he'd be gone for months. He wasn't returning her calls.

She'd climbed over the wire fence that marked the borders of her parents' land, ran out into the forest, first following an old bridle-path, then the pipeline, the sand smooth and firm beneath her feet. She stopped to catch her breath only when she couldn't breathe, lying with her shoulder blades pressed upon a bare slope of granite, her flesh and the rock made unbearably hot by the sun. If she stayed very still like the dry, pale moss and dead leaves she'd turn to dust one fragment at a time and disappear into the Earth. Nobody would ever find her.

But her stillness was jolted by a rumbling in the hollows of her lungs, coming from beneath her back. The ground shuddered in through her ears, into her molars, resonating in her jaw. It was a rock-burst. She'd grown up having her dreams interrupted by bad ground. By the hole that struck to the heart of the Earth, where good people died and others were afraid. The mine where Wycliffe Nichols said he saw the devil.

But for once, she hadn't been disturbed or worried. Instead, the thought of the unseen world just below her feet was comforting. The earth rocked her in a granite cradle, lulling her to sleep.

When she woke up, the landscape was tinted with indigo, as if her retinas had been bruised. Her hand seemed like someone else's hand as she watched it dig into the pocket of her dress, pull out a box of matches. The grating snick of the match against the strip of sandpaper travelled up her arm, stoppered by her elbow. She dropped it when the flames licked her index and thumb. The fourth match burned right down to her flesh, and this time she dropped it into a mound of dry leaves beneath a rotted poplar. As if by accident. Then the smell of smoke curling from the layer of raging life as she ran through the forest.

Roxane inhales deeply. Can she smell something, through the stench—burning hair, a copperish twinge, saline wafting up the escapeway?

Was Johnny awake when the fire cast shadows on the tarp, a magic lantern for his winding sheet, when the worms cuddled into the treads of his boots? Or had the smoke made it all a bad dream?

All you have to do is sit still, wait for rescue.

But in the meantime, the fluorescent eye of the trap door pins Roxane to the ledge. Poised upon the surface of the dark like a shipwrecked traveller clinging to a bit of driftwood that floats atop a quiet sea.

There's a rasp of boot tread on metal. A low chuckle ripples up from just beneath the light; the sound resonates in Roxane's ears. It's not until she closes her mouth that she realizes she's been laughing at herself.

Shut up, she mutters.

But she knows she'll hear the sound again before she sees the sun.

MAHAK JAIN

THE ORIGIN OF JAANVI

As I usually do on the weekends, I went shopping at Costco after lunchtime, packing the trolley with diapers for newborns, though I had bought three packs last weekend. I read on a parenting website that newborns need a change twelve times a day, and one pack contains two hundred. So a pack would last us only two weeks, and we might be too busy then to buy more. I also found a yellow pillow for feeding that I thought Sapna might find useful. I grabbed it, then I wheeled back the cart to pick up a pink-coloured spare for when the first became soiled.

After lunchtime was the most crowded time of day to shop. Every other aisle, there were sampling stations and crowds in semicircles around them. I had a quarter-slice of white bread spread with hazelnut chocolate, some coconut water, and a couple of cheeses.

Near the checkout, a woman was roasting coffee for sampling, but it wasn't ready yet. I lingered in the area, but then I saw a sign for pyjamas for women. Sapna had mentioned needing some more for after the baby was born, and I decided to pick two sets up for her.

By the time I remembered the coffee, a crowd had formed. I tried to reach for a sample, but it was impossible. An Indian woman positioned herself before the sample tray, passing the half-filled Styrofoam cups back to another Indian woman. I knew they were Indian because they were speaking Hindi to each other and when they did speak English I could hear a heavy accent. I started becoming annoyed. The quantity of cups passed back outnumbered the people the two women had with them.

The second Indian woman was taking the half-filled cups and repouring to fill each cup further. She threw away the empties and returned the full cups to her partner at the station, who then added milk and sugar and passed the cups back again. These were then distributed to the remaining members of their group—a man and three children.

The assembly line they had created had caused a jam at the station, and the woman serving was bristling—her cheeks red, her lips pressed—though she kept quiet. I was embarrassed and angry and felt the need to apologize. Then I realized that to the server I would appear to be with the Indian woman and her family, so I hurried to the checkout, my face hot.

On the ride home, I couldn't stop thinking about the shame of it. The impression it must have left on that woman—greedy Indians, selfish Indians, uncouth Indians. And who was I to argue, to try and defend, with such evidence on display? At a store like Sabzi Mandi, in Brampton—Browntown, it was called—packed with goods imported from India and even more Indians, I could laugh at something like that, but the incident made me want to erase the colour from my skin.

—∞∞∞—

When I arrived home, the minivan I bought for Sapna was sitting in the garage. She never used it, though I bought it for her to get around while I was at the lab, which I was most days. I brought in the groceries, hoping she would come greet me in the kitchen. She was on the phone, and when I heard what she was saying, I realized she hadn't heard me arrive.

I left the grocery bags on the counter. The rummaging would give away my presence, even though the garage door hadn't. I could have used a bathroom break or even a glass of water, but I resisted both urges. From the security of the kitchen, I listened to the side of the conversation I could make out.

"Mumma," Sapna was saying, "I know it is my duty. I am doing my duty. But they have kept this secret from us, it was as good as a lie . . .

"I am happy, yes, it is fine being married to him, I don't have much to complain about . . .

"But if something happens to my child, your grandchild . . . And the doctor says if my test results are not good, it could be so much worse, Mumma . . ."

I couldn't make out the rest because Sapna's words disappeared behind tears.

I didn't think that was true, the accusation that my family kept my disorder a secret. Thalassemia, that was what it was called, from the Greek *thalassa* for sea, *haema* for blood—in other words, a sea of blood, or blood infected by the salt of the sea.

The reality was that until the pregnancy, I had managed to dismiss from my mind that I was a carrier. I knew I was, of course, but the knowledge that had dogged me in Delhi had become dormant in Brampton. It was why I never insisted on prenatal testing; but then, I wasn't even aware we were trying to get pregnant until I discovered we were.

If Sapna had asked me, before we married, do you have any defects our children could inherit, I would have answered her honestly. I would have informed her that, due to a history of near-incestuous breeding in India, she, too, could be harbouring defects that would pass on to our children.

It wasn't as if I was debilitated. I had Thalassemia minor, which I hadn't worried about since I moved to Canada, more than ten years ago now, when I was twenty-one. Even the doctor agreed I was only a carrier. The anemia the disease resulted in hadn't caused me to suffer much. As I get older, my health will probably become worse, but that's true of everyone. Most of us don't know what we'll suffer from as we age.

I tried to explain this to Sapna, on the way home from the doctor's, when we had first realized the risk to our baby. "You could say that I am more prepared than most," I said. "Because I already know the ways I will suffer."

"And the ways our child will suffer?" She kept her head leaning against the window. She had not looked at me since the doctor's. "What about that?" The doctor had said that if Sapna was also a carrier of Thalassemia minor, our baby would have a "twenty-five percent chance of being born with Thalassemia major." There would have to be tests and waiting, lots of waiting, which was the part Sapna found the most difficult.

I had thought about telling her what some researchers supposed: that the disorder had stuck around as an evolutionary necessity, to keep malaria at bay. The body has a way of fighting back, I wanted to tell her. But I didn't think she would understand.

The phone call ended, and I started pulling out the groceries noisily.

"I didn't hear you coming," she said from behind.

"I just got here. I bought more diapers and some pyjamas. I can return them if you don't like them."

"That's fine."

"Were you on the phone?"

"Mumma called."

"Say hello to her from me next time." I paused, considering a bag of milk. "Actually, maybe she wants to come visit. With the baby coming so soon."

"To visit?"

"She could come on a visitor's visa." The idea had occurred to me just then. It was so obvious: Sapna's distress must be amplified by her feelings of homesickness. "She could be here before the baby's even born."

"I'll see if she wants to. My feet are hurting. Do you mind if I go lie down for a bit?"

"Of course not. You don't have to ask." When I turned around, she had already left.

⊗∞⊗

I prepared a note for Sapna on the kitchen counter: "I need to go to the lab for a few hours," I wrote. I considered adding,

"Call if you need anything," but that sounded odd. I wasn't sure what kind of salutation I should end with either. I scrapped the note and started over. "I am going to the lab and will be back for dinner at 6:30 p.m." This was better. It was more precise. "You can reach me at the work phone or on my cell." My hand hovered above the words. I finished off the note with, "Be well. Santosh."

The lab was a forty-minute drive from the house, attached to a research centre based out of a university in Hamilton. The first time Sapna had seen it, she described it as a cross between an aquarium and a mental asylum. The shelves and tables were lined with tanks of striped fish, black-and-white like old-fashioned prison uniforms, green-and-yellow like winter squash, and many such combinations that Sapna had, after her initial reluctance, come to see the beauty of. The blue-lit water and the slowly rising bubbles made the lab peaceful and meditative.

When I arrived, I felt calm and sleepy, and it was difficult, more than usual, to concentrate on the data I still needed to pore through. We were approaching the experimental phase of our research, which was on filial cannibalism. The type of fish we had selected, different varieties of teleost fish, were known to eat some of the eggs they fertilized, a form of population control. The fish whose tanks were provided with more food, however, didn't eat as many fertilized eggs. After all, there is no cost to reproducing when you are rich.

We were looking to see how the parent fish would react when we mixed in eggs fertilized by foreign fish. One would expect a poorer parent to cannibalize these before approaching its own offspring, but how would a richer parent behave?

My team hypothesized that it would behave the same as an equally rich fish that had no foreign offspring in its brood. To my younger students I explained it as a question of economics versus romantic notions of paternity. Evolution didn't hinge on or care for romance.

I had tried explaining the research I was doing to Sapna, but she was bothered that there were creatures in the world who would eat their children. "Even if it makes sense, rationally," she said. "But at least they are fish. Not like us."

"Actually, researchers are investigating similar behaviour in mammals," I had replied.

She didn't answer. Instead, she asked what we would do with the fish once the research was completed. "And all those unhatched eggs," she said. "The ones that . . . survive." I shouldn't have hesitated, but I did, and before I could speak, she had concluded the worst. "That's horrible. Even worse than what the parents do. At least they don't know any better."

Sapna and I often reached an impasse on such matters. Early in our marriage, I had tried to convince her to watch documentaries with me, mostly stuff on animals and ecology. A break from the Bollywood "masala" films she usually watched. Then we saw a documentary about dolphin poaching, and since then she had become resistant to attempts to get her to watch anything educational.

"I don't need to see how sad the world is," she explained. It was a difference between us that didn't take long to become noticeable. The fact I wanted to see things for what they were, while she wanted to pretend they were something else.

I was walking around the tanks, holding the plans of the experiment, checking again the procedural details, when the phone rang. "Dr. Santosh Mistry speaking," I said.

I received in reply a rush of wind. I glanced at the lawn through the window: the leaves on the trees were stiff and rested. "Hello?" I repeated.

"It's Sapna!"

I was frightened by the excitement in her voice. "What's wrong? What's that noise?"

"Nothing's wrong. The doctor just called—my test results are clear."

I was too surprised to answer immediately. Not by the news, but by her calling to share it and the giddiness in her voice. It was a tone she used with her friends, when they visited, or with her brothers, whom she video-chatted with every few weeks, not a voice I was used to her directing at me.

"That is very good news," I said. The wind whistled louder—maybe she was in traffic, maybe she was even in the minivan, finally making use of it. I pressed the receiver hard against my ear.

"We can talk about it more later," she said. The giddiness was beginning to recede, as if she had remembered I was on the other end of the line.

"More?"

"Yes. I have to go now. The light's changed." The phone call ended. I wondered where she was going.

That night, before we went to sleep, Sapna brought up the "more" that she wanted to talk about. She wanted me to join her at the temple on Saturday morning. Even though the baby would not be born with a major disorder, the doctor said there was still a fifty percent chance he or she would be a carrier, like me.

Praying was a habit of Sapna's, but not mine. After we married and she moved in, she set up a small shrine in the kitchen. She said she was used to waking up to the smell of sandalwood and the music of religious song, a claim I found dubious. "You did this at university?" I asked, but she didn't like that I pressed. It was a fair question: it was hard to imagine her praying in her dorm room at Queen's, which had a reputation as the biggest party school in Canada. Her experience at a university with a more relaxed culture was something Sapna and I shared in common: we had both grown up in Delhi but completed our schooling here, which was why our parents thought we would be a good match.

When she brought up the subject of the temple, I tried to formulate the kind of calm, reasoned argument that could rid Sapna of the notions of auspiciousness and inauspiciousness that she had inherited from her mother. The trouble was seeming sympathetic at the same time, which I always meant to be, but she never believed it to be true. Whatever came to mind had upset her in one way or another in the past, and after assessing the situation, I decided the best thing to do was to go along with her request as an exception.

"I'll go to temple if that's what you want," I said. The effect was immediate. She closed the physical distance between us, tucking her rounded belly into my side. She fell asleep quickly, but I stayed awake, so unusual was the feeling of her body touching mine.

⚬⚬⚬

There were many temples to choose from in Brampton, but the one Sapna attended was thankfully the most discreet, a low building that could be mistaken for an event hall. Sapna led me to the room that was used as the main prayer space. The men and women were not separated, as it was done in some temples, but sitting together in families. The room was more packed than I expected or hoped. Sapna made a path for us among the worshippers who were seated cross-legged on a large rug. A young mother was forced to lift her toddler to her lap so we could get around. "Shouldn't we just sit down?" I whispered.

We sat down at the front edge of the rug, just slightly to the right of a low stage, so that we had a clear view. The platform was about a foot off the ground: low enough for us to gaze upward respectfully but not painfully. At the back of the platform, sitting in an arc, was a family of gold-coloured statues that included Lord Krishna and Maa Saraswati. Did religion appeal to Sapna because of her education in marketing? It was, I suppose, an example of successful advertising.

The pundit arrived shortly after us, dressed in a simple yellow tunic and white pants made of cotton. He was less flashy than I had expected. He settled himself at the edge of the stage, so that his toes stuck out—if I stretched my arm forward, I would be able to touch them with my hands. An attendant leaned down to speak to him.

During that time, I surveyed the room and realized I recognized one of the men seated near the middle of the group. I couldn't remember his name, but I knew he worked at the university as well, in another department—the arts, I thought. I returned my attention to the pundit. He had started to speak.

"We are proof that God is inside each of us. And the light of God, the goodness of God, has brought us here today. Together, we will draw upon the God that is within each of us, even those who are not yet born." Sapna rested a hand on her belly.

"Together, with the combined power of our voices, we will pray for the health of the Mistry family. Their child, like all children, is a blessing that will soon be a part of us. Let us pray for the health of this child and let us give his parents strength through our prayer."

To my credit, I did consider the possibility that the pundit did not mean us, and that there could be other Mistrys present who were also expecting a child. The pundit had said "his" when speaking of the baby, and we didn't know the sex of our child, so I had more than one reason to believe this. But when I saw the soft way Sapna's hand rested on her belly and the shine in her eyes, I knew I was wrong.

Two men and a woman joined the pundit on the stage, sitting behind him with instruments. Their voices light, they began chanting, and the rest of the room joined them, hesitantly at first but then surely. The hall began to sway with singing and with bodies rocking side to side in rhythmic motions. A long time had passed since I had been inside a temple and since I had heard such collective prayers. It conjured a memory not from more recent years but from childhood: the many religious processions that had blocked my way home from school. I passed through them while afraid I would be trampled in the fervour.

The chanting and then more prayers and then some words from the pundit lasted two hours. The crowd dispersed from the rug and began to mingle. The adults stretched their legs and backs, rubbing their various limbs for circulation, while the children escaped to the foyer outside, from where every now and then came a delighted scream and the skidding of running feet.

I was proud of the control I managed. I forced myself to move as slowly as I could. I brought out the car keys from my pocket without jangling them and signalled to Sapna that it was time to leave, but she placed a hand on my forearm. She was smiling, but for the audience, not me. I found her smile nothing but cruel toward me. The pundit approached us, along with an attendant carrying a tray of prashad, food blessed by the gods.

A line began to form. I intended to move out of the way, but Sapna wrapped her hand around my elbow and held me fast. The line of congregants began to offer us their good wishes and blessings while the pundit, next to us, distributed the prashad.

The academic I had recognized from earlier approached. "Wishing you the best, Mistry," he said. I still couldn't remember his name. "I didn't know you were dealing with . . . but I hope the worst will come to pass without much ado." I nodded in thanks, as I did with the others.

When the crowd had cleared, the pundit led us through a door at the back. "It is very nice to see you with us finally,

Santosh," he said. "Sapna has been keeping us updated on your situation. You are always in our prayers."

I nodded again. Both Sapna and the pundit—whose name I realized I had never learned—stared at me, and I knew I was expected to speak. I nodded again.

"Swami-ji," Sapna said, "everything you have done for us, you don't know how much it has meant, how much more peacefully I am able to sleep at night. Shukriya. And please, accept this for the temple, as thanks from us." She handed him a thick envelope.

<hr />

On the drive home, I fixed my thoughts on the traffic lights and turn signals and road signs. The roadways here were better controlled than they had been in Delhi. The rules were accessible and easy to learn, and drivers followed them for the most part. The system worked because of a combination of cooperation and accountability. That was what allowed all of us to make our way to various destinations safely. Evidence of clear thinking and reliable procedures: this is what I was after, too, in the work I did.

I had managed to forget Sapna was even present, sitting beside me in silence, when my mind alighted on how Sapna had thanked the pundit—*shukriya*. *Shukriya* was not shuddha Hindi, a pure form of the language. *Shukriya* was an Urdu word, of Arabic and Persian origin. The two languages had muddied together and nowadays the words were used interchangeably.

"You should have said *dhanyavad*," I said.

"What?"

"*Shukriya* is Arabic. *Dhanyavad* is Hindi."

I looked over and saw that she was puzzled but still smiling.

"I would think that would matter with things like these. Isn't that what these rituals are all about? Being as pure as possible, connecting to your so-called Bhagvan?"

"I know *dhanyavad* is Hindi," she said, then paused. "Why do you talk about God like you have all the answers?"

"It doesn't take much to accept God, it seems. It's harder to speak in your mother tongue."

"God brought us together today. Everyone came out to support us. That's what God does. Thanks to their prayers, everything will turn out all right. Without God, how could we believe that?"

I was careful to keep my tone even. "It worries me that you believe this. That you think like this. It worries me that you will be passing on this kind of nonsense to our baby."

She answered just as calmly. "It worries me that my daughter's father is the kind of man who has no culture, no belief, no principles to live by. You might be a big scientist type, but as a man, you are empty."

I gripped the steering wheel, rubbing the soft insides of my hand into it. I lowered my voice. "Next time you take out that much money, you ask me first."

"This from the man who says I don't have to ask him for anything."

We didn't speak again until I pulled the car into the garage. "I am going to the lab," I said. For the first time in our marriage, I was the one who was refusing to speak to her.

I spent most of my hours in the months before I became a father in the laboratory. I watched the fish devour their unborn, and I wondered why I had married Sapna. I wondered what mistake in thinking led me to trust that our families would know that we would be a good match. It was true that the sense behind the arrangement of marriages had appealed to me, but if I had thought about it carefully, I would have discovered the bedrock of ignorance it was built on.

I first met Sapna in the lobby of a hotel, selected by her parents for its neutrality. She entered through the doors like Parvati dancing for Vishnu, rolling her hips and breasts, trying to stoke fire. It wouldn't have mattered if it had been her, or another woman my parents had selected. All I cared about was the permission that marriage would give me: to touch her, to witness her nudity, to insert myself inside her. And now, what it had left me with: to endure her. In the end, my own bestiality was to blame.

I often worked alone at the lab, the only sound the gurgling tanks. My research team, comprised of graduate and postdoctoral students and peers, was in and out, and though we exchanged notes and ideas, I perceived that, to them, my presence was strictly ornamental. I didn't know how many had knowledge of what had transpired at the temple, of my medical condition, or that I had relied on prayer to defeat genetics. That was how it would seem to them, no matter the truth. I knew what I would be thinking, were it someone else: typical Indian. I began to wonder if my team's reticence with me had always been present, or if it was something I was just becoming aware of. It was hard to be sure if my inability to form a relationship with them was a result of their suspicions about my scientific integrity or if it was simply my failure as a team leader to integrate us. It had never bothered me before, but now I felt outcast when the members of the team went to lunch together and no one asked me to join.

In my isolation, I prepared what I would say if someone brought up my status as a carrier, so that I would not be caught by surprise. It would be my opportunity to educate, demonstrate my knowledge, and remove any suspicions about the soundness of my science. It was possible, I would inform them, to prevent the spread of Thalassemia. If two carriers did not reproduce, then Thalassemia major would not occur; if a carrier did reproduce with a non-carrier, which is what had happened to me and what might happen to an offspring of mine, then the likelihood of Thalassemia minor would continue to exist, but the risk would be decreased.

I would cite the authors Verma *et al.*, who said it well in their 2011 study: "If the policy of premarital screening were to be successful, control of thalassaemia in India should have been achieved a long time ago, because this course of action has been available for decades. For the reasons given above the policy of identifying carriers and advising carriers not to marry carriers is not likely to be successful, given the current state of knowledge of the general public about science and genetics."

The reality is that India is a country that manages marriages with an eye toward economic and social shrewdness, not medical common sense. Ergo, my wife knew more about the affairs of imaginary gods than she did about blood, and the way blood keeps us chained from one generation to the next. This was why, after I moved to this country, I did an inventory of all religious iconography I possessed and threw it away. My disease was not a matter of chance, God's will, or karma, whatever Sapna might think. It was the result of poorly made decisions, specifically my grandfather refusing to have my mother tested as a carrier, despite obvious indicators, because he was afraid the knowledge would make her undesirable as a marital partner. The unfortunate situation was that this was true. Even without an official assessment from a doctor, my grandfather had to increase the dowry for my mother, to compensate for her tendency toward illness.

Armed with these facts, I felt ready for any confrontation. Even so, sometimes I had thoughts that were not suitable for a scientific mind. Sometimes I wished to return to the time when the gene first appeared. I longed to snatch it from history like snatching a pearl from an oyster, killing the host and crushing the stone into sand.

━━━⊗⊗⊗━━━

My daughter arrived in the world two weeks before her due date, but I didn't know she existed outside her mother's womb until it was already done. My lead assistant, Dr. Barry Leeds, was in my office with the initial results of the experiment. "I have unhappy news," he said. Perhaps I misunderstood his expression, but he appeared satisfied, even smug. The results disproved the hypothesis: the fish, regardless of their social standing, targeted the foreign offspring first. It seemed the fish gave preferential treatment to their own genes.

The phone rang as I reviewed the data. I recognized the number and picked up the call after the first ring. "Dr. Santosh Mistry," I said. Dr. Leeds mouthed, "I gotta go." I nodded.

Sapna's mother, Kalpana, didn't bother with a greeting, her style with me in general. She had arrived a week ago and filled my absence at home completely. "Your daughter is born," she said. "You might want to come." She spoke as if I had refused to.

I asked her to tell me more, but she cut in. "*Someone* needs to be with Sapna," she said. "She is alone."

⸺⸺

My daughter scrunched up her pink face in a bassinet in the third row of the hospital nursery. I recognized neither myself nor Sapna in her. She was small and delicate, too fantastic to be human. I had my first chance to hold her when she was brought out to feed, for only a moment, before the nurse passed her to Sapna.

"I am going to return to the house," Kalpana said.

"But why?" Sapna asked. "Don't leave me here alone."

"I won't be gone for long. We need to get things cleaned up before this one comes home, don't we?" She screwed up her face for the baby and then turned to me. "You will be here?" Her manner was suspicious. I nodded.

The hospital room was silent after Kalpana left, the only sound the soft sucking of the baby pulling milk. "She's so strong," Sapna said. She even sounded friendly. "So healthy."

We were waiting for the doctor, who would give us a final assessment. He arrived in a rush of energy, brandishing a smile like a clown's. "Congratulations to your new family," he said. "How are mother and child?"

Sapna pulled her sheet to cover her naked breast. I wanted to point out that a few hours ago she had her legs spread wide.

I had fallen into a habit of cruelty with her, a habit I enjoyed because she no longer bothered to fight back, she simply ignored what I said. The presence of our daughter stopped me.

"And, Dad, how are you doing? Any broken fingers?" I was confused until I realized the doctor had forgotten I was not present during the birth.

I laughed, though I wasn't amused.

The doctor picked up the chart. "She was born a couple weeks early, and sometimes that can lead to problems. She's a bit small, but she'll catch up in no time, especially if she keeps at it like that." He winked at Sapna, who frowned. He went through a list he must go through with all the parents before arriving, finally, at the point that concerned us most.

"About the matter we discussed a few months ago. I had warned you that your daughter could still be born with Thalassemia minor. I am happy to tell you that your daughter did not inherit."

"Hai Ram!" Sapna kissed the top of our baby's head heavily and repeatedly.

The doctor replaced the chart. "You can speak to the nurses about the exit procedure. I'll check in in the morning."

"I knew she would be fine," Sapna said. "And now you can stop fighting with me for no reason."

"She is fine," I said, puzzled. I seated myself in the armchair by the window.

"I will name her Jaanvi. As precious as life." She kissed the top of the baby's head again. "Actually, go ahead and be angry if you like. My daughter is healthy and that's all I care about."

"She is my daughter too," I said, but I felt unconvinced. It occurred to me that if Jaanvi had inherited my disease, the connection between us would have been stronger. Father and daughter, bound by blood. It was an illogical thought.

Jaanvi's lips unloosed from the nipple. Sapna repositioned so that the baby's cheek remained against her breast. The baby's eyes closed, and her breathing deepened and lengthened, then she fell asleep to her mother's heartbeat. Soon, Sapna's eyes began to droop.

I took Jaanvi from her mother's arms and carried her to the window. The code my blood could have passed on to my child was lost in the gap between generations. A perfectly normal, even desirable event, and yet, I couldn't make sense of my disappointment. I could think only of what Darwin had said, of evolution, that "non-inheritance was the anomaly."

PAIGE COOPER

THE ROAR

When Dino gets back with the guests it's dark and the helicopter's chop has both dogs crying at the door. Loyola stands up from the table to pull bottles from the fridge. The girl on the couch opens her eyes.

"You can go to bed," Loyola offers.

The girl, hair greased around her face, stays put. Dino brought her home last night.

Loyola follows the dogs out the side door. They fear the rotors about the same as they fear the vacuum: hackling and moaning at the asphalt's edge while the hired hands dart under the blades. Stein unropes a pair of chamois from the game cage. Heads loll and long black devil horns scrape the paint's gloss. He carries each in his arms into the hangar's white light, their beards dripping over his elbow. Inside, Riley's already hooked a tahr buck over the drain. The guests, disembarked, look on. The bird's still putting off a swell of fervid heat. Dino won't winch it the thirty feet into the hangar until season's end. He's clambering around in it collecting firearms and ammunition, headset collaring his neck.

"You should've seen the stag," says the man who paid. He takes a bottle off Loyola's tray.

"Twelve-pointer," says his brother. "Broadsided him on a cliff."

"Prehistoric," says the wife. Her face is lit and lined by the fluorescents. Upon arrival, she'd exclaimed devoutly through the tour of the main lodge, the cabins, the green rocky pool, every glance out over the valley bowl. Down the trail, she admired the old barn's rack and ruin. Now she stands on the hangar's stained cement with sweat on her lip and navy mascara freckling the top of her cheekbone. She flashes wide eyes at Loyola. "Just breathtaking," she says, "All those creatures out there."

"Took a shot, anyway," the man says. "Went down most of that bluff on his feet. Spent an hour tracking him."

"Who knows," says the brother.

"Bad luck," says Loyola.

"We couldn't get down to the bottom," says the wife. "The cliff."

"Couldn't see a fucking thing." The man's shrivelled smirk. That red stag's an easy twelve hundred pounds. Antlers thick as ankles. Loyola remembers him. She's not a small woman, but if she stood at his feet and embraced his neck she wouldn't reach his withers. Her fingertips spread wouldn't span the tines of his crown. No trophy for a shot like that, all the glory's in the fall.

Dino blinks all the bird's little lights off and carries an armful of slick black branches to the cage at the back of the hangar. He doesn't look at her as he passes. He replaces each rifle into its cradle, slides drawers around, bolts the lock.

Riley's already got the tahr half-naked, hide draping his knees. The paying man wants to do the chamois, so Dino hands him a skinner. Forelegs snap wet like live wood at the ankle. The pelts peel bloodlessly. Fat greases their hands. Loyola twists her own bottle.

"Never seen deer so huge," says the wife. This wife, who spent four hours in a helicopter with three men and an arsenal. She's had twenty years of this. She married a man who took her to the shooting range on their first date. She likes the soft muzzles so much she wants them in her home: clear eyes overlooking dark wood and grey slate.

"Biggest in the world," Loyola agrees around her bottle's lip. Her teeth set in the ridges of the glass. The tray cocked against her right hip.

Out in the yard, the dogs writhe around each other at the lit periphery. They aren't begging. Dino instructs the tourists without instructing them. They're experienced. They know how to slice a body hung from the ankle bones so the offal balloons from the incision like a fawn's head. The organs slide over themselves to the cement. The drain runs. Dino has the discreet authority of a butler, the woolly presence of an uncle, and the guests don't notice his corrections. Riley finds the stereo and smudges a button with a finger to clatter the steel walls with guitar noise.

The wife is watching close enough that when the men laugh she laughs. Loyola hovers back in the open air. She'll have to get more beer. A smoky breeze sneaks down through the scrub pines from the peaks. The girl's emerged from the lodge. She steps like she's passing through an herb garden in those battered boots Dino brought her home in. Her hair might be alive. When she got out of the jeep she was wrapped in a scabby fur. Dino said, "You don't want this" and peeled it from her shoulders as she twisted away. She pauses out past the dogs and their switching shadows, watching the hooked game jerk and spin under the lights. The heads hacksawed, lined up on the tool gurney like they might want to watch. The girl cranes.

Loyola crosses the yard, tray dangling, and the girl lets her approach. Loyola does not touch the bare shoulders as she says, "Go to bed. Honestly."

"Don't you hunt elk?"

"Whatever the licence is for."

"That's what they wanted, though, right?"

"Bad shot," says Loyola.

The room they installed her in last night is just a few knocks down from Loyola's own door. These are extra rooms, upstairs, barely used because the guests all prefer the privacy of the cabins. There's a black iron queen with a blue quilt and a slit-eyed bobcat treed over the mantel. Last night Loyola gave the girl a nightgown, a toothbrush, and pointed out the white towels in the ensuite. This morning, when she found the girl in the kitchen before dawn, she handed over spare clothes.

The quilt is rumpled in circles like one of the dogs napped in the centre of the compass rose. The girl goes straight to the window. In the white light of the hangar's mouth, the men stand like fangs.

Dino drives the guests out the next morning, the jeep loaded with racks and meat. Loyola finds the wife's shampoo and conditioner in the first cabin's steam shower. They smell like flowers she doesn't recognize, invasive exotics, but they're not so expensive the woman will call and ask for them to be mailed. Loyola can take them back to her room. They're for redheads and she's red-haired, though not like the wife with her layers and shades.

She sprays every surface with disinfectant. They left condom wrappers on the bedside table, the wastebasket a foot away. The paying man was smiling as she refilled his coffee four times this morning and as he thanked her for her hospitality in the drive. She drags the bedsheets off the mattress, has to crawl across the king's width to pluck the fitted corners up. His smell hides in the linen like a body in a blind. Chemical cedar. The wife's copper filaments wire the pillowcases like the remains of a gutted radio. Loyola does not seek out the spots where they soaked the sheets through, but still, she can smell what they left rising from the bale in her arms.

The only thing she finds in the brother's cabin is a tip in American singles. She pockets them. This far into the season they're still in the red, and the couple thousand from these three will splinter fast. In the lodge, she pushes the sheets into the laundry, pours bleach, and goes to the kitchen to stack half a dozen roast beef sandwiches.

Now the sun's up, soaking the mountaintops and green-heating the trees. The helicopter gleams on its pat of asphalt. The paint scratches have been polished away. She finds Riley under the hooks in the hangar, sluicing the concrete. He's too lazy to scrub. The air in here is cool with silt, paint, old meat. He throttles the water before taking a sandwich. He eats it with unwashed hands, the creases in his knuckles dark.

"You seen Stein?" she asks.

"Barn, maybe."

The dogs follow the roast beef on her plate. Down the switch-blade trail, dried hot with rusted juniper and pine sap, to the barn. Come upon it from above and it's a witch's house: steep-pitched, stitches of paint on the leeside. There's a paddock where she and Dino used to keep the horses when they ran the place by saddle. But it wasn't a barn, originally. At some point, Dino's forebears lived inside. Dino's been saying they should buy a few auction block nags. He says he misses the whickering at night. But Dino thinks money shows up as soon as you've spent it.

She ducks into the dustpit paddock and as she nears the unlatched doors Stein slides out.

"Morning." He's a skinny kid, short, the tip of a tattoo starting under his left ear. He's not breathing right. She looks at his greasy lips and guesses where the girl is.

He takes two sandwiches, one in each hand. She says, "Riley's got that west gate yet."

Stein nods as he works his snake throat. Nods and swallows. Keeps nodding, swallowing.

The doors creak and the girl joins them. Her eyes flick to the trees, the paddock corners, the sharp ears of the dogs, Loyola. She's wearing Loyola's dress: blue with white flowers, pearly-buttoned. Those boots, haydusted now, predictably.

"Morning," she smiles.

Stein closes his eyes against them both, chewing.

Loyola has never seen him embarrassed. She tips the last of the sandwiches toward the girl. "Roast beef."

The sandwich is opened like a book. The girl eats one slice of bread while looking down at the old dog, who supplicates forward on his elbows. The younger dog crouches likewise, at an hour-hand angle but just back. The girl tilts her hand, and the meat and cheese hit the ground, slick as livers in the pine needles. The girl eats the other slice of bread—margarine, lettuce. The dogs stare, arrested in half-launch. The old one's saliva droplets the dust six inches from the meat.

Loyola scratches her forehead, sweeps crumbs from the plate. The dogs don't blink, watching the girl's eyes for release.

Stein swallows one last time, wipes his hands on his pockets. "That's cruel," he says. Then he crosses the paddock, hoofs the bluff's hairpins up to the hangar. The girl turns her face to track him. The old dog passes a twitch to the younger one.

"Blow away in a stiff wind," Loyola says.

"I like them like that."

Loyola snorts.

"All wrist and ankle." The girl rocks to her toes, swings her arms to stretch, and starts for the trail up.

Her first step, the dogs lunge. The old dog for the meat and the young dog for the old. The old dog twists to run and fight at once, drops the meat, pisses on the ground. He thrashes on his spine in the dirt with the younger on his throat. The younger is snarling and doesn't let go until Loyola boots him off. White fur pink, black fur oiled wet. The old dog spiders into the pines. The younger, wet-muzzled, snaps the meat and it's gone.

Dino comes back after three. He drove the tourists all the way to the airport instead of just to town, which is all they're supposed to get with the package. He almost always does that, unless he can't stand the people, and there aren't many people he can't stand.

He's brought back groceries and two tanks of fuel. They usually tip him in hundreds. Loyola shelves cans while he opens a beer and eats the sausage she's sliced for him.

"I was thinking she'd be good on front desk. Answer the phone, greet them, get them settled."

"What desk," Loyola says from the pantry.

"You know what I'm saying."

"Sure," Loyola agrees, pulling her bag of salt forward on the shelf, tucking a new one behind it. "Pretty smile."

Dino is silent and Loyola takes the cans off the counter. She ferries two loads before Dino says, "You think she's got much else?"

Loyola lifts her eyebrows at the vinegar. He was supposed to be picking up the repaired sump pump the night he brought her home. No report on where he found her. Gas station, truck stop, diner, ditch. Barelegged with blades for calves. Veins like spring rivulets down the backs of her brown hands. Right now, the girl's asleep in the sunlight by the pool, the younger dog in sprawl nearby. She's obviously healthy. Fast blood. Curved hamstrings like she was built for flight. She would've asked him for a light or a phone call. Dino would've had to offer more. He offered Loyola a meal, which she declined, and when his came she ate half of it with grimed fingers. She remembers onion rings, a screwdriver. He drove a rusted-out Ford back then.

He says, "She mention family to you?"

"Not to me."

"We could give her a hand," he says.

"Of course," she says.

He watches her for a while, swirling his bottle. She plucks four tomatoes from the basket. He turns on the radio. She halves them, quarters them. She flicks a burner on. Why did she start cutting these? He looks out the side door to the hangar. He goes outside. Loyola twists the stove off again.

The girl picks herself up off the stone terrace when Loyola steps out into the sun. Sleeping on the rock's left red scars on the flats of her arms and thighs. The urns alongside the pool are just nameless grocery store annuals, whatever was on sale. Up here the sun is so close it thins the air dry. The stalks give up their dead easily: Loyola plucks browned florets and tucks them to decompose in their own roots. She tips water into them.

The girl trails after her. Her hair is clean now: the colour of woods before foliage. She points her face at everything in turn. Loyola pulls a limp clump, and they leave her fingers sticky and purpled. The girl snaps off something and rattles the roots doing it. She doesn't look at it, just drops the golden head on the stone. Loyola moves on to the next. The girl murders another.

"I brought you this," she says.

Loyola looks over her shoulder. The girl opens her palm. A twig. A rough-barked stick thick as a finger bone and grey with witch's beard.

"Magic powers," the girl promises. One eyebrow up, smirking.

Loyola takes it.

"You should use it," the girl advises. She pulls a plant whole from the soil, roots dripping mud.

"Thank you," says Loyola. She slides it into her breast pocket.

The girl follows her back to the faucet. The younger dog's

sucked up some new scent trail and whips back and forth in the lodge's shadow, rushing their legs. His fur is wet.

"What did he do with my pelt?" says the girl.

"It's in the rifle locker at the back of the hangar."

The dog yelps once, thrilled. The girl's fingers shred the flower in her hands. She's standing very close. "What about yours?"

Loyola picks up her watering can. "He burnt mine," she lies.

The sound the girl makes isn't audible, it's too deep in the lungs. Her pink mouth. She reaches for Loyola's wrist, but Loyola's stepped away.

The next party is four men. They're staying the weekend; they've booked three flights in the bird. They're licensed for a small massacre. When they climb out of the jeep Dino names everyone but Loyola lets the burning wind off the peaks take the sounds.

Dino introduces the girl alongside Loyola and Riley, while Stein moves luggage into the cabins. Stein's been loitering after the girl. Him and the old dog always at the edge of sight, ready to disappear. He doesn't come to sit at dinner or around the hearth in the great room when the sun steps behind the mountains.

Through the plate glass, the valley is a thick fur of pines, piebald with broadleaves and slit by the river. Loyola serves beer, coffee, whisky. The sun appears again, then moves behind the next peak. Every poplar for miles is a steeple with leaves like lit windows.

The girl sits off in one of the solitary armchairs, cornered beneath six antlered heads. Their expressions vary: some have

artful, alert ears and lifted chins, but the elder faces are dull
as barn mares. Their dusty eyeballs. The girl keeps her bottle
full between her bare knees. She is silent. She may be listening.
That's fine, the men don't want her to speak. They just like an
audience sometimes, until they don't. At that point Loyola
gets tired. "Are you tired?" she asks the girl, standing.

They climb the open stairs together. The men are watching. The girl murmurs, "What about the one with glasses?"

The men are talking about pilot licences. One of them's an
air traffic controller. One is building a floatplane in his garage.

"It's his credit card on file," is the only thing Loyola knows
about him.

"Which cabin?"

Loyola bites her smile.

"I bet he thinks I'm your daughter."

"Probably."

The men are laughing.

"He'll like that," the girl says.

The men are still laughing.

The girl jostles her shoulder against Loyola's. At the top of
the stairs, the row of doors. Loyola in one, the girl in hers. At
the end of the gallery is Dino's. Beneath them in his armchair
Dino is telling about flying through last year's whiteout, two
bears dead in the cage.

The girl says, "So it's elk tomorrow."

"Or something."

"Can I go with them?"

Loyola shrugs. She asked, once.

"I could walk," the girl says.

Loyola leans her shoulder against the frame. "There's a

trailhead past the river. Up Sawback. We could drive part of it, walk the rest."

"You want to come?" says the girl.

"I want to see his body."

The girl blinks. If she were the least bit human her wet eyes would be full of pity.

When Dino comes upstairs it's late, black in the valley and in the house. Loyola's been sitting in the glow of her little lamp. She's fingered the bark off the twig the girl gave her. He isn't drunk enough to stumble. He's led the guests to their cabins. She cracks her door when he's close. Then she widens it.

She never sees his broad face any more, she never touches his grey hair that's too long. He's always had gundog eyes and she puts her nose to the collar of his shirt so he can't look at her. He smells like he's always smelled. He never stopped smelling this way, but he stopped letting her get close enough to know it. It's painful, how familiar he is. Her memories are accurate, even if they're used ragged.

"What?" he says. She stays close under his chin, out of sight.

She kisses his throat. With his hands inside her shirt his mouth becomes less inhospitable. She is steady and silent. She used to voice eagerness. Then she learned to conceal herself in the underbrush, let him track her down. Lately, she's been waiting months, seasons, this dry summer at least.

The girl's little stick, lost on the bedspread, jabs her. She'd rescue it from snapping under them, but her hands are busy. She arranges them, moves on him. He grips to slow her down but she refuses. He comes loudly, even though next door the girl is or is not listening.

Loyola pulls away as he takes in air. She could lay herself down beside him like she used to and let all his circling mongrel thoughts thicken the air. Instead she brushes away the snapped halves of the twig. In her bathroom she runs water like she's killing his scent, clearing the mess. But she doesn't step under the jet. She stands lock-kneed on the tile with him all over her.

Outside, there are bodies under the trees. Split hooves and missing skulls, bones jawed open by opportunists. She's found them deep in underbrush or at the foot of high places. She walks whole days. She finds a few every season. Never any antlers. She can't tell. She couldn't say for sure. Who else would come all this way but their guests, their dogs.

When she comes back he's gone. He's draped her pelt over the quilt, fur down, a skin waiting to wrap her. She's always been free to go.

At breakfast the men are mouthy over coffee. The one in glasses is grinning his stupid secret away. The girl doused him with herself. He must think he split her open. Dino is all anecdotes and wisdom. He smiles at Loyola when she refills his mug. She walks back and forth, bringing hot things and removing what's finished.

In the kitchen she fills a cooler with sausages, cheese, hard-boiled eggs, bread. Dino comes in. He strokes her waist. He puts his nose to the back of her neck and breathes against her vertebrae. He kisses her skin.

She stays still until he goes. Then her knees sag. Her mouth opens. She folds against the cabinets, forehead to the wood, battered in the chop.

In his room, she does not touch anything or inhale. This

room, the master, built when they first conceived of this life. Not horses but helicopters. Rifles and racks for tourists. They sold twelve strong mares too cheap at auction. They didn't need all the extra acres of conifers. Loyola slept in this wide bed. She crept from it every morning to percolate the coffee. He's left it immaculate.

The spare key for the gun locker is jumbled with some others—the generator shed, the jeep—in a drawer.

The girl comes with her to the locker, a chain-link partition at the back of the hangar. Loyola skims the black barrels. The girl goes straight for her pelt, stuffed into an empty shelf. It has no arms or buttons, no collar. It's short-haired, rough, built on summer. In this light it's the colour of dead leaves. Its underside is wet-white with grease, like he peeled it off her an hour ago. The girl folds it to her chest, bends her face down to rub against it.

Stein and the dogs stare at them when they come out into the yard. The side door hangs open. The sun's been up for an hour, but the light's still choked pink. The valley's hazy with forest fires. Later, in the worst of it, they'll all wake bleeding from the nose, desiccated, and Loyola will wash bloody sheets every morning.

Stein's mouth moves as he calls to them. The old dog wags low, once.

As Loyola turns the engine the girl rolls her neck to look at the lodge, the cabins, the flowers lining the pool. She doesn't see Stein where he stands. "Slaughterhouse," she mutters, leaning back into her seat.

Down the valley, across the river, to the trailhead. The path is dry, scraping along at the spine of the Sawback peaks, a root-bound stepladder climb between aspen stands. It's not quiet. There's a roar. The red stags don't bugle like birds, they make a meat eater's sound of want.

One of them sounds, miles off.

Close, an answer from a larger set of lungs, a fuller-maned throat.

The girl's grin widens. Loyola keeps climbing. The girl bounds ahead, hair sweating to her skin.

Loyola keeps her eyes on the cliffs, and the bottoms of the cliffs, for his branched antlers. He'll be his own gravemarker. They found him where he grazed. And the shot, if it hit, hit the hollow behind his shoulder blade. He tipped starboard, overcorrected, and then toppled. His landslide body. His feet at gallop down the shale. She'll find his corpse at the bottom splayed by petty birds. Or else he walked away.

When they reach a bluff, a scoop neck between peaks yawning east over the foothills, they stop. The girl picks at her buttons. The borrowed jeans come off, the wet shirt. She's stout, naked. Her sunburnt clavicle. She holds up her fur and flaps it. In the smoke it's roan red, speckled down the haunches, paler in the belly. She turns into it, smiling as she shivers its fatty lining over her shoulders. The forelegs ribbon down between her breasts. Loyola reaches to pull the girl's hair out from under the pelt and smoothes the lock down over one shoulder.

A stag roars eastward. Loyola jerks. That was his voice. The one who fell, or didn't. There he is.

Beside her, the yearling doe with her long neck and soft muzzle flicks her ears and stamps her four fresh legs. She's taller than a thoroughbred, black eyes already distant with alien concerns. She steps into the trees, crackling dead sticks, branches brushing her flanks and waving in her wake. She moves slowly, but she's gone.

The road back to the lodge is rutted with smoke. The dirt widens into the drive before the rippled skin of the hangar. Loyola comes around and the young dog runs the older right under her wheels. His body is a jolt. She stops. Kills the engine. The younger wheels away, shouting.

The old dog is dying as she gets to him. His feet scrabble but it's just his broken back finishing off. She touches his swivelling ears, then carries him to the hangar. She has to check. She heaves him up to hang and slits him to drip. The younger is hiding. There are a hundred places. The woods, or under the veranda. She follows the smell of him down the trail, into the old barn, and finds him in the box stall, backed up under the feed trough, growling like a meatgrinder. He is wet-mouthed and serrated. His throat tears rabid threats. He'll chase her bleeding through the woods. He'll find her by her screams. He'll pulp her soft face and pull open her throat. He'll drag her down and dye his muzzle in her rib cage. Has he ever killed anything? It doesn't matter.

She puts the skinner into him under the edge of his skull and he shakes down to the hay, eyes straining at her. She carries him soaking hot back to the hangar to heave him up beside the other. Her mouth is dry. She is panting. She splits his belly, lets his lungs, bowel, stomach slop on the shop floor, cuts off his paws and peels his fur face. She flaps his bloody pelt off his body. His dog body. Nothing but dog.

SOUVANKHAM THAMMAVONGSA

MANI PEDI

The bright industrial lights hung in neat rows on the ceiling. And afterwards the sadness settled in Raymond, in his body. It went all over. Heavy. He couldn't lift his arms or his head and couldn't see his opponent's face or understand what he was doing in the ring. He couldn't think out there. Couldn't move his feet fast enough, couldn't move out of the way when a punch came. The punches landed in the middle of his face. Quick, hard, sudden. He saw it coming and he was trained to see it coming but he stood there like some fool just waiting for it. But it wasn't him. It was the sadness. The heaviness of it. All over his body. In the review tapes you'd see the punch in slow motion, how it waved through his nose, his cheekbones, his temples, his ears, his hair like he was ocean. And when it was over he could see nothing but black light. He had to get out of it and he knew it for some time. He was just there for someone to punch through, a body to pass on the way to some victory belt. He had become what they call a trial horse. He said he'd quit if it ever got to be like that, and it got to be like that. It wasn't the best way to go out but to go out was all he wanted.

So that's why he got into the nail thing. It wasn't something he wanted to do. The nail thing. He was scooping out ice-cream flavours at the mall and when that shift was over he was stir-frying bland bean sprouts and cabbage. His sister was the one who got him into the nails. She lived in a big house with her unemployed husband and four small children. They could afford for her husband to be at home because her business did so well. She owned Bird Spa and Salon. The slogan was "Nails! Cheap! Cheap!" It was catchy. She said Raymond didn't have to go to school or nothing. He just had to listen to what she told him to do. It was just like it was in the ring. She'd yell at him like he was in the corner and he'd just go out and do it.

His sister didn't want him living where he was, in a mouldy, cold basement with just one window. When he got the place he thought he would be able to see sky once in a while, but the floor wasn't down low enough and all he saw were shoes and boots and heels. Feet. No glimpse of sun or sky at all. He was feeling sorry for himself, as if he was the only one who ever lost a thing in the world, but that wasn't true. It was his sister who came to get him. She was real dramatic about it. She had a key to his apartment and kicked open the door and beat him on the chest, saying even if he didn't want better for himself, she did. She brought up their dead parents. She always did that when she was desperate to make a meaningful point. She said they didn't leave Laos, a bombed-out country, in a war no one ever heard of, on a raft made of bamboo to have him scooping out ice cream or frying cabbages with old grease oil. So he joined her at Bird Spa and Salon just to get her to calm down about it all. Not long after that, he was answering the phones and saying, "Hello, Bird and Spa Salon. We do nails. Cheap! Cheap!"

At first he mopped the floor, filled the bottles with nail polish remover, cuticle oil, or whatever it was that was running low. He cut hand towels into neat little squares to save everyone time. He turned on the switch to keep the waxing oil hot. When all that got to be easy for him to do, she asked him to sit in and watch whenever the girls did manicures and pedicures or waxed an eyebrow or upper lip. It amazed him to see people transform so instantaneously. They came in looking sad and tired and exhausted but left giggling and happy and refreshed. He thought of the injuries he'd caused in the ring when he was younger, just starting out. There was the guy who didn't wake up until a year later or the guy who lost his confidence, stopped training, and ate doughnuts all day and let himself lose his shape and lost his whole career. He thought of seeing only the black light and waiting for the black dots to disappear. Waiting for the bell to ring so he knew they were into the next round. Boxing was just sad and tired and exhausted, the way he knew it.

When one of the girls who had worked there quit on his sister because she had a bad cough that wasn't going away, and his sister could do nothing to help her, he was given his own station. The first thing he did was put the plastic basket of supplies and lotions to the left of him. She didn't like that. "What the fuck, Raymond. You going southpaw on me now. You a right-hand. All your supplies go on the right. Fuck! Maybe you shoulda thought of that when you were boxing.

You know how fucking southpaws are hard to fight—they do everything backwards. It's too late, isn't it. To go southpaw now." Raymond didn't say anything. He just moved the basket to his right. It was easier to do.

His sister had him practise on some plastic hand dummy. Thing was, it wasn't attached to anything. It was severed at the wrist and stood straight up like it was high-fiving. The plastic hand could be moved around for a better angle to paint a heart or put on dots. His sister watched him without saying a word. Then, she picked up the plastic hand and waved it in his face and said, "But hands come with fucking bodies! You can't be turning them three hundred and sixty degrees to draw a fuck-ing heart! And is that what this is supposed to be, Raymond—a fucking heart? Looks to me like a stinking blob of disgusting shit." She plopped the plastic hand down and held out her own hands. She wanted him to practise on her. For someone who did manicures all the time for other people, his sister sure didn't have the best nails. They were too long and yellowed at the tips. Her skin was dry and flaking. It was like watching a dentist with tartar-stained teeth preaching about flossing and brushing often. "Watch your fucking face! I know what you're thinking about these nails. If I paint them, the polish remover I use on clients will just fuck them up. And I ain't going to use that gel shit on myself. It's fucking expensive." He started to cut her nails, when she added, "And you have to talk to me like I'm your client. Most of the time they won't talk to you because they think you don't know how to speak English, which is fine because it's exhausting to make conversation. I don't care about their kids or husbands or boyfriends or what the fuck they're doing this weekend. If you don't want to talk to a client because you're tired or not interested, just turn to me and speak Lao. They'll think we're talking about them and that'll shut them right the fuck up." For cheap nails, Raymond had to do and remember so much.

Most who came in were patient with his mistakes. Many came in with chipped polish on their nails and he would remove it. The clients liked that this big, burly former boxer was handling their female hands. He thought they might be uncomfortable with a man handling them this way, but they only thought it was wonderful to be touched by that kind of muscle in so gentle a manner. Raymond was good with the endless repetition and assessing what needed to be done. It reminded him of sparring at the gym, having to think quick, act, respond, handle the situation, anticipate what was coming. No one client was the same, but there were some basic things everyone needed. He removed polish, cut nails, applied cuticle oil, and pushed skin away from the nails, to give it a clean look and shape. Some nails had no shape. They came out straight and flat on the nail bed and he had to round them with a file. The file moved around the corners of the nail and he had to work the file at a forty-five degree angle, deciding where on the nail it should begin to bend. It was very subtle, the bend. He wore a mask at first to cover his nose and mouth and he wore gloves too, but he couldn't get a proper grip and couldn't converse with his clients so after a few days he removed them and exposed himself to those tiny shards of nail dust that entered and scratched at his lungs.

There were so many colours. He couldn't get his head around it all and remember them so he just told his clients to pick a colour once they walked through the door: Shrimp

Sunday, Funny Cool, Double Personality Blue, Alter Ego Pink. The names and colours went on along and all around the walls. Because he was a man and because it was so unusual to see a man doing nails, the clients gave him large tips, twenty- or thirty-dollar tips, while the girls in the spa got two- or three-dollar tips. They told him the tips were to buy something nice for his little lady, take her out on a date or simply because they enjoyed a good flirting. His sister, one to always notice things, said, "Fuck! Shit! I don't get those kinds of tips. It's because you're a fucking man, isn't it? Men. Even in a business I own myself and built up myself, we are still paying them more. And these are women who are doing this. They should know!" And she'd mumble something while he counted his tips, which added up to more than what his sister charged for mani-pedis.

It was the toes he despised the most. After only a few weeks of working on them, he got warts on his hands and had to take a few days off. His sister said, "Shit! I ain't gonna let anyone see that ugly shit while you're working on them. Plus, it might be contagious. I don't fucking know. I told you to wear gloves!" Raymond didn't like arguing or talking back to his sister. She'd always taken care of things and of him. Even though it wasn't the greatest place to be working, it was a chance to be with family. She talked tough and was for real tough, but she had a good heart. It was possible to be both.

He picked at a wart on his hand. "You ain't gonna quit on me now because of this, are you? You know people come in just to see you. They love seeing a former boxer painting nails at the salon! They all ask for you. And those tips you get. They're something special. Never seen anything like that."

But it wasn't the warts he was worried about. Warts weren't so bad as mumbling nonsense and bad headaches and black lights or being dead. Warts went away eventually. That didn't bother him. It was the smell of feet. It was like it got into the pores of his nostrils and grew there, like a follicle of hair. It was becoming a growing part of him, the smell. He could never forget what he did for his living because it was always there. Not even when he was cooking or eating would the smell go away. It got to be that he was beginning to taste the smell of feet at the back of his throat. It smelled sour, a little like bleach. It also got to be that he didn't enjoy food either, which made him lose a little weight and this made his sister tell him it was a good idea since it made him look good and that meant more clients coming in to see him. But it was not the women. He blamed this smell on the men. Most women took care of themselves. Their toes were clean and taken care of to begin with, years of salon and spa visits. It was the men who came in, who had never had a pedicure their whole lives and wore heavy socks and leather boots year-round. Ones who had been too embarrassed to show their untreated toes to a female pedicurist. As a man, Raymond knew not to mention or speak or acknowledge the mess, the years of neglect and abandon just because the feet had been out of sight. The layers of skin he had to slough off like cutting a slice of butter. His sister would say, "You know why the skin there is yellow? Well, the fucking guy pees in the fucking shower! That's why. Disgusting fucking hell!"

Well, they were not all disgusting. There were some favourite clients like Miss Emily. He didn't have much to do when she came in. Her cuticles were already peeled back and her nail bed was long and thin and smoothed. The skin on her hands and feet felt like a baby's. She would always do him the courtesy of removing her nail polish so he could start on the filing and paraffin wax and then lay down the three layers of polish. The first layer was to protect the nail from the polish, then there was the polish colour itself, and the last layer was to help from chipping and to keep it shiny. His sister—and sisters do know their brothers well—watched him closely and said, "What, you think you got a chance with that Miss Emily there? She's rich and educated. None of the things we are or are ever gonna be. Don't you be dreaming, little brother. Keep your dreams small so life don't ever hurt you and spit you out with your innards all hanging out for all to see. It just ain't ever gonna happen. Keep your dreams small. The size of a grain of rice. And cook that shit up and swallow it every night, then shit that fucking thing out in the morning. It ain't ever gonna happen. If there's something I know in this life, it's rich women. And that woman ain't for you." But even when someone talked him down like that, Raymond just kept at it. When he didn't see Miss Emily, he painted and shaped all his clients' feet like Miss Emily's. If he could get the nails looking like hers, anyone could be like Miss Emily. And like everything else in this life that could be true, his sister, the older one, the one who had been around longer and knew better, as much as he hated it, he knew she was right.

One day, Miss Emily was seen at the door of the store with a distinguished man. He wore a three-piece suit and had polished black shoes and despite the smell of feet, Raymond could smell the man's cologne. It was not one of those drugstore scents. Raymond would know about them. He had tried them all. Miss Emily stood at the doorway with this man and in his smell she disappeared as if a dark cloud moved in and covered up all that was bright and good about her when she was alone.

His sister saw his face fall, the way it fell in the ring when he knew he was losing. After, on the drive home to his same old place, she said, "Raymond. Didn't I tell you. You've got to not have dreams. That woman ain't gonna love a man who does nails. Just ain't gonna happen. You're given a place in this life and you just do your best in it. Fucking give it up. I hate when you get like this. Plenty of girls for you! They want to get with you all the time, but you don't let yourself see it. Like the girls at the shop. They're all wet for you."

Those girls were married or serious with someone. What his sister didn't know was what they talked about behind her back when she went out for a smoke or when she had to go out and get supplies. How they tried to get pregnant but none ever caught on because of the chemicals. How their coughs started and didn't ever stop. Even if this dream about a Miss Emily was not his to have, he thought it was nice to have it anyway. He knew it was naive and not real worldly like his sister was, but this little dream was his, and it was decent. This idea that someone like Miss Emily could love him. Raymond, not one to speak up to his sister but this one time, said, "Well, you know, maybe Miss Emily ain't ever gonna be with a man like me but I want to dream it anyway. It's a nice feeling and I ain't had one of those things to myself in a long time. I know I don't got a chance in hell and faced with that I wanna have that thought anyway. It's to get by. It's to get to the next hour, the next day. Don't you go reminding me what dreams a man like me ought to have. That I can dream at all means something to me." And his sister looked away from his face. His face looked like hers but beaten and beaten up. A crooked nose, a busted eyebrow with the hair not meeting in the same place. Although her face was treated to facials and creams and anti-wrinkle serums and was smooth and glowing, she felt like Raymond's face, beaten and busted, and she just didn't want to look at that face hoping. Hope was a terrible thing for her—it meant it wasn't there for you, whatever you were hoping for.

She took out a cigarette, lit it, and fumed at the mouth, while he stared down at his palms where the warts were coming in again and would put him out for a few more weeks. As they sat there in silence, in the oncoming darkness, their car windows were open. They could hear a family in their backyard, somewhere nearby, the sizzle on the barbecue, the sweet smell of steak on the grill, and the giggling. It was the kind of giggling they themselves did as kids. Now, that kind of giggle seemed foolish for them to do. It was like a far distant thing, a thing that happened only to other people. All they ever could do about it now was to be close to it and out of sight.

COLETTE LANGLOIS

THE EMIGRANTS

31.03.2070 station 1 / If you come, bring bamboo.
Last night I slipped under the cover with James, and though he didn't say anything—hadn't been able to speak for days—a slight pressure when our arms touched answered he felt me there and was glad.

Then I thought of the bamboo sheets I once owned, their soft weight both warm and cool, their spring fern colour and faint wooden scent. I can't remember whether they ended up at the Salvation Army thrift store or in one of the boxes that went to the salvage area at the dump with all the other too-heavy luxuries we couldn't take with us. We who made this one-way journey stopped talking about things like that when we realized it was a kind of torture for each other, and those kinds of memories were best kept to ourselves.

James is dead. Sometime in the night two of us were breathing, then only one. That faint contact of skin when my arm nudged his as I lay down was the most we ever touched. I can only hope my presence in those last hours brought him some comfort.

Later I'll put him outside with the others, but for now he's lying where I left him, under the weightless silver sheet. Even after thirty years I still hate those flimsy covers, reminders of long ago over-baked potatoes. I refuse to call them blankets, whatever their little yellow labels might say. The product of some mind that thought the only purpose of blankets was to keep us warm.

The responsibility of reporting now rests with me. The complicated processes we once used to choose a successor each time a lead rapporteur died—usually culminating in acclamations, rarely a secret ballot required—all seem so quaint now. Our concern for fairness, avoiding unnecessary conflict and hurt feelings. How important those things seemed when there were more of us. By the time we were down to four we settled it with a crib tournament. James and I went with rock-paper-scissors.

No contest this time.

I'm writing in the garden, the only place I can stand to be now. The fibre-optic strands funnel in the scant sunlight, and the plants give off a slight humidity that makes breathing just a bit easier. They grow surprisingly well here, as I expect James documented in much more technical detail. Aside from the cold, the red planet is naturally kind to them, with plenty of subsurface water and minerals in the dust that, mixed with our compost, provide all the nourishment they need. About the garden: I should tell you a few things, in case James forgot to mention them, in case you come and no one's left. For example, it is important to blow on the carrot tops. In the still air they droop, weakened, until they touch the ground and turn yellow. But a little breath, like the breezes from home, seems to give them the strength to grow sturdy and green.

I will do my best to remember anything else that you might not think of on your own and leave notes for you. Just in case.

I'm dreading moving James's body. For one thing, it means putting on my space suit. Also awkward and silver, like the sheets. It has always annoyed me that everything in space is silver. As though all the imagination got used up on the mechanics of things, with nothing left over for colours and textures. He's light enough after being sick all these months that I could probably carry him, but I'll use a cart anyway. It wouldn't do to throw my back out, being alone.

I'll need to be much more careful from now on.

I'm back in the garden, and it's done. James is outside with the others. The botanist has joined the two medical doctors and gaggle of engineers frozen naked and staring empty-eyed up into eternity.

And then there was only the psychologist.

The most useless and unskilled of the entire group, but someone at Headquarters must have thought it would be a good idea to include one. Five hundred years ago they would have sent a Jesuit along on an expedition like this, but in 2042 they wanted a PsyD. And now here I am. Who would have bet on this old girl to be the last?

About the arrangement of the bodies: Headquarters told us to preserve them for future research, but they didn't give specifics. I wonder what those hypothetical future researchers will make of our artistry. Maybe they'll think we invented some new religion, when the truth is it was only a mix of aesthetic pleasure-seeking and boredom. We started out lining them up, but later someone—I think Sonny, the water engineer—had the idea we should arrange them in a circle, with toes touching. Back then the circle was only a little more than half formed. Now there's just one wedge left, for me, although I don't know how I'll get to it when the time comes.

I took my time getting ready to move James. The death-smells of emptied bowels and decomposing tissue, I'll be honest, made me retch, but I lingered anyway, knowing these would likely be the last human odours I would ever breathe, apart from my own. Outside, I jumped on his knees to break them so his legs would go straight like the others', and when they cracked under my feet I nearly threw up in my helmet. I should have positioned him when I first woke, when he was still a little warm and the rigour had not yet set in, instead of wasting time writing and crying in the garden. I would say I'll know better for next time, but there won't be a next time, will there?

It's occurred to me I may seem a little flippant about James's death, and I apologize if anyone's left who cared for him and is offended, as unlikely as that is. After all, those of us who came on this one-way trip were chosen partly for our lack of human ties to the blue-green planet. Enticed here by adver-tisements hinting at adventure and new beginnings, perhaps not unlike those that lured my third great-grandparents from England to their Saskatchewan homestead two centuries ago.

Though James and I were alone for over a year, I still feel I hardly knew him, and for that I'm sorry. He was a soft-spoken man. He had a wife and child once, I think, killed in a car accident on a Florida holiday in the 20s. He liked spinach and backgammon. I will miss him.

About the bamboo: I don't expect you to bring all the machinery and materials to make sheets or even to know where to begin with that whole process. We'll find other uses, food to start, though I admit I like the idea that one day, even after I'm gone, bamboo sheets will exist on the red planet. I can't say what insights and lucky coincidences and inventions will be required between now and then. I just have faith the mere imagining that something's possible can be enough to set it on the trajectory to being. Like Da Vinci's helicopter sketches. They waited four and a half centuries on paper, but the day came when they flew.

Anyone reading this should be aware there won't be many more messages, maybe none. The solar cells that power the transmitter are failing. James noticed and warned me about this a few months back. At least the water and air systems are holding, even though all the parts were supposed to have been replaced years ago by later missions. The ones that never came, let me remind you.

"Delayed" was the official word. "Budget cuts" the truth, revealed in one final unsigned message, right before Headquarters shut everything down. After some discussion, we agreed to keep that last transmission a secret to avoid getting anyone else in trouble. However, after revisiting the issue with the surviving red planet settlers, i.e., myself, I've decided after all this time to spill it.

Whichever board or committee made the decision to cut us off knew it was our death sentence. Of course, they also knew they could get away with it. Who would have bothered to organize protests and petitions? Who would have cared, given our lack of human ties to the blue-green planet?

All I want is some shred of accountability. I don't expect you to do anything about it now, but it makes me feel better to know you know I know. If you're even reading this.

That's all for now. The carrots need my breath. / cmb
Send

Red Jacket, Assiniboia East. September 8, 1885

Dear Sister,

I regret I have not been able to write to you since my last letter from Montreal. We have had much to do to secure provisions and make a cabin livable for winter, which our neighbours who arrived two years ago tell me is fierce and long in this part of the country. The journey was as the agent forewarned: the prairies seem endless, days and days to cross by train, and, I'm told, they continue days more to the west of us all the way to the Rocky Mountains. For now, we live under a warm sun and cloudless blue sky, with green and golden fields all around save a stand of trees they call cottonwood along the small creek that runs nearby. Your nephews are growing strong with hard work, fresh air, and sunshine, and your nieces lovelier by the day as every breath fills their lungs with Nature's raw beauty.

Lucille is finding the conditions harsh, I fear, and suffering for the lack of female company. I assure you the cabin is no poorer than some of the lodgings you and I knew in our childhood, but it must be remembered my wife was raised with more comforts than you and me, and it is to be expected she would find this change in her circumstances difficult. I thought she was bearing it admirably until the last of our trunks arrived and we discovered the one containing all the quilts, so carefully stitched over countless evenings, had gone missing. I do believe her heart broke at that moment. In a poor effort to raise her spirits, I joked I would ride off every dawn to hunt buffalo and wolves until I gathered enough pelts for us all to have as fine sleeping robes as any Sioux chief, but I fear this only caused her more distress. I am sorry necessity required me to trade Mother's little pewter pin box, among other small treasures, for a few of the Hudson's Bay Company blankets. I do hope you will forgive me this loss. Our new blankets are plain, but made from heavy wool that will keep us warm in our beds through the winter.

I must end here, Dear Sister. The trader who has kindly agreed to deliver this letter to Moosomin Station will soon depart. I trust you and Jimmy and my little nieces are well and wish you good health until I may write again.

Your devoted brother,

J.M.B.

08.04.2070 station 1 / I saw what you did.

I'm not even sure where to start this report now. From the beginning, I guess.

The latest dust storm ended overnight, and today I was able to get out to complete all the routine checks and maintenance. The winds were especially fierce, and the cleanup took much more time than usual. First, I climbed the outside of the dome over the garden to sweep off the solar panels. The station's layout from that perspective reminds me of a medieval cathedral, one that endured extensive additions and renovations every hundred and fifty years. A few saints and gargoyles would fit nicely. My dusting job worked: the lights have stopped flickering now.

Next I went down to the main roof to inspect for the beginnings of fractures or other damage. Nothing to report. The robots who assembled the station before our arrival clearly took pride in their craftsmanship. They've all long since been pillaged for their parts, donating their vital organs to keep water pumps and climate control systems operating. To keep us humans alive. I know they weren't sentient (I haven't gone crazy, if that's what you were thinking), but it seems unfair to me how they ended up despite all their diligence and industriousness.

After the roof, I walked the building perimeter. No damage to the walls either. They are smooth and the same silver as my suit, designed to be easily visible from approaching vessels—the ones you never sent. They glow reddish orange in the faint sunlight.

Last, I visited each of the solar panels arrayed around the station. Again, no damage, just in need of cleaning. All the storage cells are in good shape, except for those connected to the transmitter. Very little charge left—this may well be the last time you hear from me. If anyone's left to hear. After what you did.

By the time I finished my spit and polishing, sunset was near and both moons had risen. I checked on my fellow settlers, also dusty, but otherwise as I last left them. The summer breezes will blow them clean again.

Eight women and eleven men, a mandala for the stars to gaze down upon. The oldest ones, from twenty years ago, are desiccated but otherwise intact. They will start to thaw in a few weeks, but in these anaerobic conditions they don't decompose, and most nights they will refreeze anyway. No wild animals to feast on them and scatter their bones. No worms to eat them from the inside out. They will be here like this until our swollen red sun swallows the solar system, then explodes everything into stardust to start it all over.

I have a childhood memory of a brief stop on a long road trip at a graveyard somewhere between the Qu'Appelle and Assiniboine rivers, near the Manitoba border. Weathered tombstones, some sinking into the soggy ground, others toppled over on their faces and lying under two inches of water. Wind snaking through the flooded grasses and shaking the tops of the cottonwoods. Somewhere beneath the watery surface, the blind, muddy bones of ancestors born on the other side of the Atlantic, who once must have found solace standing or kneeling in that quiet patch of earth on the outskirts of their village. As we who came here found solace in our mandala.

I still had nearly an hour of oxygen left. I lay down in my wedge as I sometimes do and nudged my frozen neighbours in greeting. The twenty of us all together again. The mandala complete. Jupiter rising between the two moons, and the shimmer of the terrifyingly near asteroid belt between us and our giant neighbour.

Spring is here and the days are lengthening. About −10 degrees now, quite bearable compared to the typical −103 winter's day. If only I could take my suit off.

Spring. Olfactory memory is the strongest and the most easily recovered. I conjured up the smells of late April on the blue-green planet. Fresh grass in wet peat. Melting dog shit. Half-decomposed leaves. Thirty years, with no idea what spring smells like here. If I ever do find out it will be with my last breath. Death by hypercapnia, which I imagine to be quick and painless although I don't know for sure, since none of us went that way.

They screened us for suicidal tendencies, of course. Even now, despite what you did, I have no intention of hastening the end of my life. I am far too curious about the possible endings to this strange story of mine, and all the moments in between.

But if there were a way to arrange it, if I could be sure I was about to die from say, a massive heart attack within the next 120 seconds, and if I could only have the time to strip naked, then hold my breath long enough to run out the door, lie down, and get into position with the others, I would. From my place in the circle I would open my eyes wide and inhale through my nostrils, sacrificing the few seconds I might have had remaining just to grasp that one last bit of knowledge.

The blue-green planet twinkled a few degrees above the horizon, becoming brighter and more distinct as the sun sank and disappeared. I lifted my hand and waved with my clumsy silver arm. On the way here, if you can believe my naiveté,

I imagined a crop of fashion designers inspired by our expedition—for a brief time before our departure we were minor celebrities—creating new and improved space suits in a variety of colours and cuts to flatter various body types to be sent along with the next vessel and with each vessel to follow. New trends for every season. Well, it was a pleasant thought for a while.

As I lay in the mandala, imagining the scent of the red planet spring and sleek fuchsia space suits, Earth suddenly shone bigger and brighter than I had ever seen it before. An illusion created by the dust still floating in the meagre atmosphere, I thought, but alluring nonetheless, like a candle in a distant window on a black, pre-electricity night. Then there was a moment when awe and wonder at the loveliness of it switched to horror as I realized what you must have done for that to happen, right before the starburst flash, brief fireball, and complete darkness.

Twenty-three years since I last had news of you, I have no idea what unsolvable political crisis or technological fuck-up could have made blowing up the entire planet inevitable, but I have to tell you, from here it all seems pretty unnecessary. I guess I'm in shock.

I wonder if the moon is still there, and what will happen to it now. Catapulted into the sun, flung into outer space, or left to inherit the blue-green planet's orbit and continue its silent path in peace?

I am going to send this. I waited. I considered. Here it is: even if there is only the most infinitesimal chance someone is still left to read this, sending these words is the right thing to do. Whether or not anyone receives them is not my concern.

I wish someone would breathe on me the way I breathe on the carrots. / cmb

Send

Red Jacket, Assiniboia East. 12 April 1889

Dear Sister,

My news is sorrowful, and I pray you do not find yourself alone as you read it. Yesterday we buried Lucille. Her heart failed her, the doctor said, though he had no need to tell me. To think she would have had her fiftieth birthday this September. Though I often feared for her when she was bearing our children, always mindful of how you and I lost our own dear Mother, once our last was born I imagined she was safe and we would grow old together. How foolish I was.

Poor little Leo is inconsolable. Being the youngest, he was still accustomed to clinging to his mother's skirts and climbing into her lap, an indulgence for which, I now regret, I often reproached her. Amelia and James have taken him and Sarah into their home, where they will stay until after the harvest or perhaps longer. It gives me some comfort that, though deprived of their Ma, the littlest ones will know at least the care of their gentle sister. The others will remain with me to help ready the fields and sow the crops, which must be accomplished soon, the land and elements caring nought for our grief.

She is laid to rest in the yard of our new little brick church, I assure you, as good a Christian burial as she might have had in England. My neighbour the Swede built her a coffin from lumber that I believe he had intended to use to repair his barn, and would accept no payment in return. His wife brought us breads and stews made in the style of their country, and was most kind to the children. It grieves me Lucy never sought to befriend her, nor the German ladies who live nearby and who, when they learned of her passing, also came to clean the house and attend to us. Though their English is halting and they do not share our faith, they are of good heart and would have made her fine companions. All of our fellow countrymen regrettably dwell at some distance from our little homestead.

The coffin was plain but well made. It only pained me to think of sweet Lucy lying on its bare wood, and, as there was no finer fabric to be had for a lining, God forgive me, I placed inside one of the Company blankets she so detested. Aside from you, Dear Sister, only Amelia knows, and like me she thought it was the best to be done for her mother under the circumstances.

I am told the Reverend spoke well at the service, though I confess my head was so filled with other thoughts I hardly heard him or recall what he said. The little church was full of our friends, and even our Catholic and Lutheran neighbours came to pay their respects. Two young North-West Mounted Police officers who boarded with us for a few days when they were caught in a terrible blizzard last winter, on hearing of our loss, rode up from White Bear Post. In their fine scarlet coats they made a handsome addition to the funeral procession. I am certain Lucy would have been pleased.

I fear in some of my letters to you I have written things that may have cast my dear wife in an unfavourable light. I beg you to put those out of your mind as the unkind thoughts of an impatient and obstinate husband. I have had no true cause to judge her so harshly for her unhappiness here. She was raised a merchant's daughter, with many comforts, and had just hope and expectation of living her days as a merchant's wife. She was so until the decision, which was my own, and taken with greatest insistence, to uproot us from our homeland. She bore me fourteen children and was a most devoted mother. Though, as you surely remember, we both grieved deeply the loss of brave Henry at the brink of his manhood, I daresay it was she who comforted me more than I her in that darkest of times, when I could not find rest for the dreams of my beloved son sinking to his death in the Pacific. It is I who am at fault, having brought the sorrows of these recent years that broke her dear heart upon her, and for this I must and shall beg forgiveness to the last of my days.

Dear Sister, I am sorry to write with such melancholy, but I trust you of all people will grant me your pardon, for like our dear Mother you are disposed to see the greatest and most good in all, and possessed of a patience and understanding your wretched brother could never hope to find within himself.

I enclose a letter Lucy wrote only a week ago to her friend Mrs. Anson, and ask that you would deliver it in person along with the tidings of her passing, as I fear the dear lady will be most grieved. Perhaps you would also be so kind as to call upon Lucy's brother Charles and his family. Though I will write to him myself, I would wish you to convey my respects with the kindness and sympathy only you could.

Your devoted brother,

J.M.B.

12.04.2070 station 1 / I've been practising.

I count to ten, take a deep breath, open the door, and run. So far I've only been able to get about two-thirds of the way to our wheel before I can't help myself and let the air out. I blame it on the suit. Awkward and clunky as it is, it slows me down. Naked, I think I could get there in time, but I need to be sure.

As if this whole plan weren't already complicated enough, I thought of yet another problem after my practice run this morning. Most of the surface is fine dust and quite soft, but there are pebbles and larger rocks, some of them with razor-like edges. The smaller ones are what I worry about, because they're harder to see and shift from place to place with the wind.

My conclusion: I don't think I can pull off complete nudity. I might need my boots. I picture myself almost making it, then puncturing the ball of my foot on a sharp stone, crying out— and you can imagine the rest. The researchers would find the mandala with its one empty wedge and nineteen peaceful bodies almost god-like in their serenity. Nearby would be the corpse of a naked old woman, awkwardly clutching her foot and her face contorted with some mixture of pain, surprise, and profound disappointment.

No, I don't want to be that woman. I still have some sense of dignity. So in my breath-holding practice I must factor in a few extra seconds to take off my boots and toss them away before I get into position.

I am well aware the odds are close to nil that I will have the just-right notice of my impending death, which will allow me to even attempt carrying out this sequence. But if it happens, I intend to be ready.

After my practice, I repeated all the routine checks. I have been experimenting with changing the order of tasks to get through them more quickly and was pleased I set a record today: four minutes and fifty-three seconds less than the previous one. It's not an obsession with efficiency, only that at seventy-something years of age, I would like to conserve my energy where I can. In any case, no structural damage or systems malfunctions to report. I will say now, conclusively, the transmitter batteries are completely gone. I held out some hope they would recharge at least a little after my last message, but after several days they fail to show the faintest sign of life.

Why am I still writing? One could say I went ahead and sent my last message, even after what you did, out of shock, with my internal processing of what had just happened incomplete. But I'm beyond that stage now.

Perhaps a sense of duty. We were, after all, sent here at considerable expense with the expectation we would notice things and report them, making our contribution to the collective knowledge of humankind. They screened us for qualities like diligence and responsibility. No social loafers on this mission. Given the slightest possibility someone survived total destruction of the planet and, even more improbably, was still picking up the signal, simple duty demanded I send that message.

But now? Now I no longer even have the means to transmit, yet I continue to write. Could I really still be clinging to some fine thread of hope? If someone survived the explosion of the blue-green planet. And if that someone received my final transmission. And if that someone had a way to travel here. And if, when that someone arrived, I was still around to let them in the door or they had the wherewithal to figure out how to open it themselves. And if they found this room and the systems were still functioning, so my words were still on this screen. Then . . . what?

I tug a little on that fine thread and it stubbornly refuses to break. Am I deceiving myself into improbable hope, not wanting to admit I am only clinging to a habit, some vestige of normalcy in the face of a really fucked-up situation? Could it be these words are just a pathetic attempt at sorting out my thoughts, at maintaining sanity with some reasonable measure of comfort? That in the end I write only for myself?

I have no answers to these questions.

I have been lying in my little wedge in the mandala. It may seem morbid to you that I spend so much time with corpses. I, too, might have thought so once. When I left the blue-green planet, in my country it was customary to dispatch the dead to morgues, funeral homes, crematoria, and to leave the handling of the remains to professionals. Perhaps an afternoon or two might be spent in the company of an open coffin with the loved one's embalmed shell inside. Cosmetics artfully applied to give a semblance of peaceful sleep. More often a closed casket, or not even a whole body, only a small urn of ground bones and ash.

It was not always so. Once, in the not-so-distant past, bodies were laid out on kitchen tables, where they were washed, groomed, dressed, cried over by family members. Homes were small, and all the daily activities of cooking, bathing, nursing infants, mending clothes, conversing must have gone on all around. The men of the family, or perhaps a kind neighbour, would have built the coffin from whatever lumber was available, and loved ones would have laid the body inside and nailed it shut. There might have been an undertaker to dig the grave and cover it over, but even that task was often left to the mourners.

I was forty-one when I boarded the ship that brought us here. My parents had died in a plane crash when I was still in grad school, I was ten years divorced, had no children, no siblings, and had lost touch with any remaining aunts, uncles, cousins. Lack of ties to the blue-green planet.

Headquarters deserves some credit. They did at least put substantial thought and effort into selecting the right combination of people. Not only complementary skill sets, but a balance of gender, personality traits, values, interests. For the most part they succeeded. We were a remarkably harmonious group. A real community. Of course there were some limits. Most importantly, they screened us for fertility—a test I passed with flying colours, thanks to a hysterectomy two years earlier. As cold and indifferent as Headquarters could be, even they understood the absolute horror it would be to allow a baby into this living experiment.

So you see, this is my family. When I lie in my little wedge I feel no horror or revulsion toward my dead companions. Rather, I take comfort in their presence, the feelings and memories that resurface, the smiles and tears they bring. I have tapped into that ease and understanding of life and death all my ancestors must have had until a mere century or so before I left our planet. Here, in my part of the mandala, I feel only a sense of belonging, of being in my rightful place. Of being home.

There is one more observation I need to record. When I was looking up today, toward the dusk horizon where the blue-green planet should have been, I saw something. A handful of faint twinkles. I noticed them yesterday evening too, but today they are slightly bigger and I am certain I did not imagine them. They are approaching. Perhaps some of the debris field, a few molten rocks that will collide with this ball of red dust and complete your destruction. Or, dare I hope, perhaps a handful of ships carrying survivors. And bamboo.

Either way, I will be ready. / cmb

Red Jacket, Assiniboia East. October 24, 1889

Dear Sister,

I received your letter some weeks ago, and regret I have not been able to reply sooner. The harvest demanded every ounce of my physical strength so that, hungry as I was, for weeks I often fell asleep mid-supper and had to be nudged awake by one of the boys to stumble off to bed with my belly only half-full. The wheat was plentiful this year and the prices fair. I am relieved the children will all have new sets of clothing, those of the youngest having become quite threadbare with use. It pains me my dear wife is not here to partake with us in this long-hoped-for bounty. She might at last have allowed herself a few small luxuries, and perhaps her hopes might have been rekindled and her spirits lifted by the sights of the full pantry and all her brood in tidy little trousers and dresses trundling off to the Sunday service.

Your words as always brought me great comfort. It eased my soul to read that Lucy, though with some trepidation, also approached our journey with a measure of excitement and anticipation, and not merely in obedience to her husband's stubborn will. I am grateful she so confided in you, and that you have seen fit to now share those confidences with me.

You asked, most delicately, if I might in the next year or two remarry. I think not. Lucy's memory is yet too dear, and I should hold myself content to dwell with it alone to the end of my own days, though I suppose this causes you some concern for me. You wrote of our father remarrying in less than a year, I think, in your kindness, to assure me it would be no disrespect to Lucille were I to do the same. He was younger than I, and ourselves much littler, when he and Maggie were wed. Even were I of a mind to take another wife, there are but a few unmarried ladies dwelling nearby, only a widow or two who I should not think suitable due to age or temperament. The children are mostly old enough to see to the running of the household, and where there might yet be want of a mother's hand, Amelia has supplied that of eldest sister with such grace and gentleness as would have much pleased Lucille. You should not think even me helpless in these matters, Dear Sister. When Mother was ailing, was it not I who let you suck my little finger while I rocked you to sleep, cooked porridge for the rest of us, read stories aloud, and yes, even combed and braided my little sister's hair! Of course you would not remember yourself, but I assure you it is the truth, and our siblings will bear me up should you doubt me.

You also asked if I might now return to England. The answer, Dear Sister, is no. As I have written, the land is at last yielding us some profit, and I have hopes our continued industry and determination will see us to greater, though still modest, prosperity in the coming harvests. In any event, it must be some years before I should have the means for us all to cross the Atlantic again, even were I to wish it so, and I do not. Rather, it pleases my heart the children have set down little roots of their own here, like the tenderest of carrots in early summer, and I would not now pull them from this earth.

I confess I, too, in spite of all the losses and hardships we have endured, have grown to love this soil. When we first alighted from the ship in Montreal, the thought came to me I should never set foot on such a vessel again, nor suffer the reeking ports and grey seas I had so come to despise. The fiercest of prairie blizzards could not change my heart. Those dark waters that took our Father and Mother to their early deaths and lured my beloved Henry to the farthest reaches of the globe only to drown him, I should never again take their salty stench into my nostrils, nor bear their fetid touch on my skin.

I have instead discovered a new ocean, one of blue skies and swaying gold and green. I have discovered my home. Of course you should always be welcomed with joy and warmth in any home of mine, Dear Sister, should you and yours ever be moved by some calling in your hearts to join us. On many a dark eve I have placed a candle in my window with a thought to you, perhaps at that very moment climbing from your bed to glimpse the same stars disappearing below your horizon that now rise over ours. Often now I recall the years when you and I and our siblings shared table and bed. I think on the small rooms that once contained the whole of our family, and how strange it seems to me that our children are separated by a vast ocean and hardly acquainted, and our grandchildren never likely to meet. I suppose it must be that they too will venture forth someday, to search out their own homes under these boundless heavens.

Your most affectionate and devoted brother,
J.M.B.

ANDREW MacDONALD

PROGRESS ON A GENETIC LEVEL

My brother and I tried to divvy up the depressing tasks ahead of us. He told me I should fetch our mother, who had all but given up the English language for Ukrainian. My brother thought that because I worked with more Ukrainians at the security agency than he did at his bank, I spoke it more frequently and could better articulate the reasons why she should come to our father's funeral. In exchange, he would tell our uncle he wasn't allowed to attend the service.

"He mostly speaks Ukrainian too," I said, balancing the phone between my chin and shoulder. In the mirror, my reflection tried to figure out the best way to tie a Windsor knot.

"He'll be angry, and I'm bigger than you. He'll break your skull."

Our uncle Joseph had been a boxer once. My brother wrestled in college, at his peak placing third in the Pac-10 conference's one-hundred-and-seventy-four-pound category. The idea was that they could cancel each other out.

Joseph wasn't welcome because our mother claimed he'd done terrible things to her when she was little, before they emigrated from Ukraine. Nobody in the family knew what to think, whether he did or didn't. Our mother's mental illness made it difficult to judge. For our father, there was no ambiguity. A year before he died, he drove me to a steak house and, after we ate, showed me a gun he bought, which he intended to use on Joseph.

"I'm going to go to his house and blow his fucking brains out."

One can see why my father's heart exploded. Though technically the product of calcium and protein and fat forming a brick of plaque in his aorta, his end represented the metastasizing of years of suffering, the day his body could no longer host his sadness.

In addition to not speaking English, our mother hardly ever left the house. Her apartment was in a dreary part of Toronto, in the neighbourhood we all used to live in. Her entire floor was filled with Ukrainians. One storey down, mostly Sudanese. Upstairs, Mexicans. The property managers liked to rent whole floors to families who knew each other, so that if one tenant couldn't pay rent, the others would chip in. It was communism on a microscopic scale.

I knew she wouldn't let anyone in, so I used the key I found on Dad's keychain. I had the black mourning dress my brother bought for her draped over my shoulder, encased in a skin of crinkly plastic.

"Hello?" I said, opening the door just wide enough to slip in.

The apartment smelled the way my mother smelled: like smoke and some sort of vinegar. Eucalyptus plants, steroid creams for an imagined skin condition, the bleach she used on the linoleum of the kitchen to keep it chemical-white.

"I'm not leaving," my mother said in Ukrainian. I traced her voice to the dining room, where she was drinking coffee and having a cigarette, crocheting a complicated pattern into a doily.

"You need to get ready."

"Are you dead?"

Instead of answering, I took the dress and set it on the chair next to her.

"Nicolas bought this for you. I think it's your size. Try it on."

She shook her head.

"Your father and I hadn't spoken in months. The last thing he said to me was that he was selling our *Encyclopoedia Britannica*." The doily had the look of a jellyfish in her hands. "There's coffee over there. Some left for you."

Pouring myself a cup, I marvelled at the artifacts of my childhood that still hung on the walls. It was like being in a museum with a wing dedicated to myself. Pictures of my brother in his wrestling singlet, performing an arm-drag takedown on a weaker opponent. Peacock feathers we collected during a family trip to the zoo, arranged in a petrified fan shape. And there we were in a sepia-toned photo, a family. My brother, me, our parents, circa mid-eighties; tan lines, Dad's glacially receding hairline, surrounded by a frame made of cherry-coloured mahogany, the gilding a brassy yellow.

"You need to go," I told her. "He was your husband. You never got a divorce."

"A technicality."

"Your wedding ring is still on."

She looked down. "I've gotten too fat to take it off."

Sighing, I went to the bathroom and called my brother. Without much thought, I rifled through the medications behind the mirror, silently noting unfamiliar names. My brother answered.

"How are things on your end?"

"She's not coming."

"Why not? Did you show her the dress?"

I asked if he wanted to talk to her. "You can try to convince her."

For the next ten minutes, I listened to her switch from English to Ukrainian, shouting sometimes, turning away from me so I couldn't hear what she was saying to my brother. I went to the living room, turned on the television, and watched some soap opera without the sound on. The plastic cover of the dress I'd brought crinkled, and I turned to see she was holding it up.

"It's dowdy," she said.

She sighed, pulling the zipper of the dress down. She held it to her chest, the bottom half falling past her kneecaps.

In the car, she asked me if I was still dating Maria Teodorowycz, the daughter of someone on Mom's floor in the apartment building. Maria was a geologist who measured the levels of chemicals in soil that corporations sent her. She and I had gone on three dates, had sex on the last one, and then . . . I don't know.

"Doesn't Tina have a friend you can see?" Mom said.

Tina, Nicholas's wife, wanted nothing to do with me.

We drove in silence for a bit. She put her hand to her face and blew on the window until a patch of condensation formed on the glass.

"Did he feel pain?" she asked, turning down the radio. "Do you know?"

I repeated what Nicholas had told me.

"The doctors said it was slower than most people imagine. That he probably felt everything breaking down." Some urge to punish her made me pause before adding, "Like he was having a stick of dynamite going off inside of him."

She looked at me, her makeup starting to smear.

"Why would you say something like that?"

Nicholas was the first person the hospital called, Dad's primary contact. I remember what I was doing when he called me in the same way I remember what I was doing when the first airplane crashed into the twin towers.

I was making rounds as security for a computer-parts warehouse. Normally I didn't answer my phone, since it could get me fired. All it would take would be one blink on the security cameras. But my brother rarely called me.

"Dad's had it," he'd said, just like that. Not, Are you sitting down? Not, Are you ready for catastrophe? "Arterial thrombosis. Think of taking a baseball bat to the heart."

I stopped walking around the warehouse and turned off my flashlight, which left me alone in a blurry half black. My father had a very gentle appearance, the sort of soft, smudgy face that had the peach hint of a child's pastels. He never drank and never smoked. How does a heart go like that? These are things you think about.

He had been driving a truck of anti-freeze and felt his heart tighten, and when he felt the life of him being squeezed like a balloon in a fist, he pulled over.

"They said if he hadn't pulled over," Nicholas told me, "he could've killed a lot of people."

That night I had a dream where Dad was an infant and I was holding him, in the apartment from our childhood years. That he melted to death right in my arms, and that I tried to contain him as he became liquid, slipping out of my grasp but leaving no wetness behind.

In the car, Mom popped in the electric cigarette lighter, wiping her eyes on her arms and on the nice new dress Nicholas had bought her.

"You know, he had one testicle," she said, snorting the pain back through her nose and into herself. "Did you know that?"

"Can we not talk for a while?"

"No, no, listen. In a way, you and Nicholas being born was a miracle. The doctors said he had a better chance of being eaten by a shark after getting struck by lightning. You know, when I got pregnant, I thought I had cancer of the ovaries or something. Even when they did the . . . what is it . . . the ultrasound, I didn't believe it." She lit a cigarette. "They had to cut you two out of me, since my uterus had a funny shape. So it's two strikes against you, and here you are anyway."

The funeral home was also run by Ukrainians. Everyone we knew who died ended up having their viewing there. My best friend got a brain tumour after high school and ballooned up with water from the drugs. He'd been put to rest in this funeral home. And then the old woman who'd lived at the end of the hall, who nobody was related to, who blessed pregnancies and told everyone she had been the first woman bicycle champion in Europe.

We pulled up and Nicholas was standing in the front with Tina, who hung on him, dripping with beauty and perfection. She waved when she saw us.

Mom and I stared at her through the car window, through the caked blots of velocity-crushed insects. I looked over and saw that Mom's hand was white, gripping the door handle the way she did whenever she was in a turning vehicle. We were combating the same gravity, the same physics.

"I don't think I should be here," she said, adjusting her seat belt so it held tight against the throat.

"Me neither," I said. "But here we are."

Once we got out, Nicholas shook my hand and Tina hugged me, and then they did the same thing with Mom. Tina smelled gorgeous and rekindled that hole of loneliness my therapist said might always be inside me, no matter how I tried to fill it.

"How are you holding up?" Nicholas said in Ukrainian.

"I'm sorry for everything," Tina added, in a broken parody of the language that made me sick to hear. She sounded like Dad did whenever he tried to speak Ukrainian, his accent, as Mom described it, a stone bouncing around in a washing machine.

We all went as a unit into the funeral home. Even though Dad hadn't been Ukrainian, the priest we got was. He shook our hands and I thought he held on to mine a bit longer than was necessary. He saw Mom and they spoke quickly, in a dialect I couldn't follow.

They stopped and the priest took a deep breath. "It's good to see you, Lena."

She took a deep breath too. "Let's get this over with."

Dad told me he wanted to be cremated, and apparently told Nicholas something different. He was dressed in his wedding suit—Nicholas's idea. A lot of the people in the viewing room were new to me, truck drivers and mechanics Dad worked with. Rough-looking people in suits that didn't fit them properly. I felt their discomfort. Also people I passed in the apartment building whenever I visited Mom. Dad had been an only child and our grandparents on both sides were dead, so the only family there was were me, Nicholas, and Mom.

People ambled around. Nicholas gave a speech in English, I gave one in Ukrainian. Mine was short: this was my father, he was a good man, he died something like a hero. Mom wept, and at some time during the speech I gave, I wept too. Tina wept, and in a shameful way her sadness warmed that hole my therapist told me I had, filled it with heat. I was in love with her. Something. It wasn't very important.

We went one by one to see Dad's made-up face, his fantastically gelled hair. He had been carefully shaved and smelled like plastic.

"Is it like a painting?" Mom asked. "Can I touch it?"

"You can touch him," Nicholas said, putting his arm around her shoulder.

She started touching him as if she were blind and judging the shape of his face, slowly, then spreading her entire hand over his mouth until it was a flattened spider. Someone from the funeral home came over and asked kindly if she could not do that.

"Now you," I said, patting him gently on the shoulder first, getting harder until I was almost slapping, "you can fuck off and let my mother touch her dead husband."

Before things escalated, Nicholas stepped in and pulled me outside.

"Can you relax?" he said. "I can't hold it together for everyone. You need to do your part."

There was a generosity of spirit in the way he said such things, and that generosity extinguished the warmth Tina had kindled in me. I thought: Who was this person, instructing me on being a proper human? Once, our mother had tried to kill herself by taking too much of her medication. Nicholas did nothing. He just started crying. I had to call the hospital and sit on her chest and slap her face so she wouldn't go into a coma.

I related this piece of family history to him. "Do you remember that?"

Nicholas grimaced. "I was seven."

"I was seven too," I said. "Now, if situations had been reversed, and you'd been the one trying to keep her alive, would you have had the emotional wherewithal to go to college, get a good job, fight off the world and your personal demons? Would you have your beautiful life, or would you be working in a warehouse and hating yourself?"

He stared at me for a while. Finally he said, "How long have you been waiting to say that?"

"Forever, fuck face."

"Aren't you just a sad, lonely narcissist."

Comments like that can only be made by people you love. Only someone you love knows how to make you hurt like that. It's natural to want to hurt them back, and that's what I tried to do, in a physical way. He put me in one of his wrestling holds and kept me in a sort of homoerotic body lock that made me feel naked and defeated.

"Are you done?" he asked.

"No," I said, and he squeezed my ribs until a wisp of air forced itself out of my nostrils. "Yes. Please. Put me down."

It took me a while to regain my composure. The lack of oxygen had made my brain constrict in an unnatural way. I eased myself back into the wall and slid down it like a gob of spit until I reached the ground.

"Two things," I said.

Nicholas sat down next to me.

"What?"

"Do you think mental illness is hereditary? And does Tina have a secret twin somewhere who could love me?"

Getting on in years as we were, we sometimes talked about genetics and DNA, what sort of fuckedness we'd inherited. The first psychiatrist our mother had seen diagnosed her as manic-depressive, the next called it narcissistic personality disorder. That same year, *The Diagnostic and Statistical Manual of Mental Disorders* removed narcissistic personality disorder from its pages. It just ceased to exist. So she went back to schizophrenic.

Sitting against the funeral home, Nicholas and I discussed whether one or both of us would, or already did, suffer from a genetically inherited form of mental illness.

"People whose parents are depressed are something like twice as likely to be depressed," I said.

"True. But this is circumstantial." He meant that the trauma Mom probably had experienced as a little girl had been the cause of her instability.

Over the course of our shared childhood, our mother had attempted suicide, stolen cat food from stores, had sex with someone who wasn't our father. Some days she was beautiful, just a gorgeous person, a gorgeous presence in our life. Ukrainian isn't a particularly melodic language, but you would weep to hear her read poems from her homeland.

But there was also the ugliness, the cracks in the fresco that was her also. One time we were even taken out of school by social workers because Mom had crushed up some of her antipsychotic medication and put it in our orange juice.

Nicholas reached over and put his hand on mine.

"She has a friend," he said, and at first I mistook his meaning. I thought he meant Mom had a friend. He clarified that Tina had a friend who might be predisposed to liking emotionally damaged adult-children.

"You'd hit it off," Nicholas said.

"What kind of rear end are we talking about?" I asked. "I'm in the market for asses shaped like globes."

"The kind that belongs to a woman. That's all you need to know."

While we were outside, Mom had one of those moments where she left the world of human beings and entered the world of animals. She fell down in the middle of talking to a truck driver who worked with Dad.

The driver said, "He had a picture of you, from when you first met," and then he showed it to her.

Mom was in a bikini, Dad was without a shirt. Luminescence bounced off them three feet in every direction. Mom's fall was like a crumbling Doric column, just crippled her from the toes to the shins, up the legs, knees, pelvis, spine, until she was a collection of pieces on the floor, wrapped in that black dress with the makeup smears.

"Can you take her home?" Nicholas asked, and I nodded, buoyed by the moment we'd recently shared outside. I felt my perception change. Instead of being angry that I'd swallowed all of his trauma along with mine, that his life had eclipsed mine in all-important categories, I suddenly saw him as an example for me to follow. I was like a tram that just needed to align myself on the same rails he rode on.

Mom got into the car and I buckled her seat belt.

"I almost married a gay Jew," she said. "But your father fixed my car and took me away from my world."

I drove her back to her apartment, the place she hadn't left for weeks before her estranged husband had died, driving a truck.

"Come up," she said, pressing the elevator button.

She told me she had been seeing the ghost of one of her dead neighbours, that she sometimes thought there was a worm in her ear, inserted via a bloodless surgery by someone malevolent, and which she tried to soak out with Epsom salt baths. By the time we got to her door, I had a glimpse of what it was like to be her, living alone in the apartment.

To even the confessions out, I told her I hadn't been with a woman for three years, and that for a while I had developed a substance-abuse problem.

"Cocaine, mostly," I said, mentioning that I'd checked myself into a detox facility, where I dreamed I was my brother. "Sometimes I think he dreams he's me. That's for a good laugh."

We got to her door. I had the sense the words she had spoken to me, and those I had spoken to her, had pressed together like palms.

"I'll visit more," I said.

She shrugged. "If you think I'm going to commit suicide over this, you're kidding yourself."

It was shortly after this that I decided to visit my uncle Joseph, probably to kill him, or at least do something irreversibly damaging to his face with my fists.

I tried to enlist my brother, since two nephews are mightier than one.

Nicholas nixed the visit.

"He'll cripple you," my brother said.

"Not if I cripple him first."

Joe had spent part of his youth in the Soviet Union, back when the Soviet Union was still the Soviet Union. He had been hardened under extreme, politically dangerous circumstances. I was under the impression he'd once killed a man with his bare hands. My brother and I were only the sons of immigrants; the hardness had been lost between generations. Some residual hardness perhaps existed in my brother, which accounted for why people respected him more than they respected me.

Tina also vetoed the decision. I'd wanted to go do this thing together as brothers, in a Shakespearean way.

"Think of it as destiny," I said.

She shook her head at me.

"Don't ruin things," she said. "You just want to destroy him the way you destroy yourself."

Walking me back to the car, Nicholas told me not to take what she said to heart.

"Her hormones are all janky. We're trying to have a baby."

I stopped.

"You didn't tell me."

My brother looked at his hands, fiddled with his wedding ring. It shone in a way that was somehow light and sound, a shockingly bright "ting" that made me blink. He seemed to be beaming the reflection from the gold band directly into my retina.

"I didn't want to depress you," my brother said.

"Depress me? I'm going to be an uncle. How is that depressing?"

I smiled and waited for Nicholas to smile.

"She told me she saw you take the knife."

I had taken one of their knives, intending to carve a new hole in our uncle.

"Your wife is a liar."

Nicolas sighed. He could see the outline of the knife against the inside of my pocket. Without looking him in the eye, I handed it to him, pinching the blade and giving up the handle.

I hadn't seen my uncle for years, not since the psychiatrist unearthed the sordid details about him from the Pandora's box of Mom's subconscious. He was, to use a very Nicholas term, a *persona non grata*.

It took a while for me to drive to the apartment complex where he lived. On the way, I wondered to myself whether I would, in the end, be capable of killing someone else. I waffled. At a stoplight, I conceded that breaking my uncle's ribs might suffice, maybe break a few things of his. "You will vacate your place in my dreams," I told my dead father, who always appeared to me in my sleep, asking me to avenge all the wrongs committed against my mother.

A tired-looking teenager let me into Joseph's building. Walking down the hall, I noted a piece of the paisley wallpaper curling and, with impotent anger, pulled as much of it off the wall as I could.

I knocked and a woman came to the door.

"Is Joseph here?" I said in English. She looked at me blankly, so I repeated the question in Ukrainian. "I'm his nephew."

"He's out," she said. "He should be back soon. How do I know who you are?"

I showed her my licence. She nodded and moved aside. I followed her to the living room, to the television set.

"Are you his girlfriend?" I asked.

Instead of answering, she said, "No smoking in here. We're trying to quit."

She sat on the couch and turned on the television. I walked to the kitchen and poured some water into a Mason jar I found on the counter. Particles in the water swirled like the flakes in a snow globe.

"That's a very nice suit," she said when I rejoined her in the living room. I was still wearing my suit from the funeral. "What kind of work do you do?"

I told her I worked in finance, with money.

"It's very lucrative."

The best revenge I could think of, to enact both on Joseph and a universe that could allow him to exist and do the things my mother said he did, would be to make love to this woman.

The thought was ugly and, for that reason, compelling. I waited for an hour, with her, this woman who had some kind of relationship with a monster.

She switched the channel to something about nature and plants. The odour in the room developed pungency, a mix of both our scents. The program was describing a fungus that took over the brains of ants and brewed an insanity of such magnitude that the ants kill themselves. Excusing myself to go to the bathroom, I took the long way, through the kitchen, even though she'd instructed me on how to get there. I passed by several serious-looking knives, attached to the side of the cupboard by two powerful magnetic strips.

Any one of these would do Joseph in, particularly if he never saw it coming. I decided to wait until after I had pissed to select my weapon. Relieving myself, I thought of the ants, of the fungus, of my brother's unborn baby, with whom I could fashion a version of myself that was utterly unlike my current sense of identity.

I could be funny, make jokes, bring him gifts to win his affection. I could also try to develop a closer relationship to my mother. I finished pissing and made all of these resolutions with an optimism I had no right to have. The woman in the living room didn't get up when I left the apartment. I'm pretty positive I passed Joseph in the hallway. The parking lot had expanded to the extent that it took me a long time to find my car.

My brother's light was on when I drove back. Through the window, I could see dinner in progress. He waved at me. He took the napkin from his collar, all spread out to catch any food that spilled, and folded it with alarming delicacy. Before he opened the door, I willed myself, on the level of my DNA, to mutate. When the door opened, I believe I became, at least for the moment our lungs swallowed the same square foot of air, a very good thing.

J.R. McCONVEY

HOW THE GRIZZLY CAME TO
HANG IN THE ROYAL OAK HOTEL

One day a bear got loose in the Royal Oak Hotel. This was in the early years of my employment there, shortly after my discharge, when it hardly felt real to be out in the world. They were using the lobby to shoot a film that featured a grizzly bear attack, and while it could have been done digitally, the director was a blowhard who insisted on bringing a real bear in from the Yukon to preserve the authenticity of the scene. So I guess you could call what transpired poetic justice, if you believe justice ever reads like a poem, or that any true poet would take carnage for a muse.

On the day of the shoot, there must have been a dozen experts and handlers crowded into the palatial main lobby, with tranquilizer guns and cattle prods at the ready. None of it mattered. Three days prior, the bear had been plucked from its surroundings, from the woods and the water and the ambient scent of prey, and herded into a cargo plane for a quick flight across the continent to an urban nightmare. It was just too flabbergasted at the drastic change in its environment to remain docile. As soon as the klieg lights were turned on it, the bear went berserk, storming around the lobby, mauling two guards and a production intern with running swats that looked tossed-off, just-for-the-hell-of-it, then stampeded the craft services table and knocked out the lights and began doing furious laps in the darkness. In the chaos someone managed to corral it into Banquet Room C and barricade the doors with a sofa, giving everyone some time to attend to the injured and work out what to do next.

They might have ended up resolving the situation rationally if the congressman hadn't been staying at the hotel. He was visiting from down south to gauge support for a pipeline project—a man known for loud suits and louder opinions. As soon as he heard that the grizzly had run amok, he made it his business to intervene. When he stormed into the trashed lobby with his sleeves rolled up, grinning and talking at inspirational volume about "the proper way to deal with this kind of a situation," it was as though Palm Sunday had come early and here was Christ preaching his way into Jerusalem, vowing to throw the thieves from the temple, a camera crew trailing like the faithful behind him.

The congressman intended to shoot the bear. To a man of his sensibility, he said, it was absurd that the animal should be given consideration; he'd seen what the beast could do (though in fact he hadn't been there for the ruckus) and believed that as long as it was alive, it presented a significant danger to the public, which he simply couldn't permit on his watch. That's when he pulled the vintage Colt single-action .357 Magnum revolver from the holster on his belt and told the cameras that with the expansion bullets he was using, he could drop the bear at twenty paces, no problem.

It was clear right away that the congressman couldn't be allowed to just kick down the banquet room doors and open fire on the bear. Objectors said a game warden was the proper man for the job, or animal control, but they were shouted down; since the congressman had turned it into a news event with political implications about the city's ability to protect its own, it was impossible to deny his request outright. The manager of the hotel stepped in, ostensibly to express outrage, yelling righteously and pointing out that it wasn't even legal for the congressman to carry his gun here. But you could tell there was more to it than that: he felt like he was being upstaged. As manager, he said, it fell to him to make decisions about the bear. Furthermore, the Royal Oak promised the highest-quality luxury hotel experience, and he insisted on taking full personal responsibility for such a gross inconvenience to his guests.

The two men went back and forth for a while, and my attention wandered, as it often did at work. I don't remember how long it took them to decide, but I can remember exactly the moment when I saw the manager turn and point at me.

The manager knew my situation, and enough of my history that I guess I was an obvious choice. I stayed quiet while he explained how he couldn't risk physical harm to himself at such a crucial moment, when so much depended on his being able to coordinate the public response once the inevitable questions started flying. I thought about my sister, all she'd done to land me the job, when he said that the hotel's reputation was at stake, and how of course they couldn't expect an esteemed guest like the congressman to carry the whole burden of this errand on his own. I knew better than to protest when he started talking to the camera about heroes and casually dropped a reference to Afghanistan, as though it were a dash of exotic spice, something to sprinkle on his speech for flavour.

It was enough; he didn't have to mention the other things—Kandahar and the detainees and the tribunal and my time at the veterans hospital—for me to understand that I wasn't being given a choice.

I remember thinking how this was all just another day to them, as if it were the most sensible thing, as though the hotel lobby was the scene of such spectacles all the time and if they just put their heads together and stayed the course, everything would turn out all right. You could see the fever in their eyes, though, the tremor in their hands—the need to inject the venom they'd created into someone else, distancing themselves from the threat while heightening the drama, making a better story. They needed a soldier, and here I was.

The beginning, at least, was all worked out beforehand. I would accompany the congressman into Banquet Room C as an official representative of the hotel. My role was to cover the congressman while he took down the bear and to intervene only in the event of an emergency. I was issued a shotgun, a Remington 870 pump-action 12 gauge, personally delivered by a VP from the GamePro Outfitters Group of Companies, who wished to provide whatever aid they could to help end the crisis. They put me on camera holding the gun while the GamePro rep joked how it was the fastest, most powerful choice for getting lead into a bear that was coming at you with a chip on its shoulder. I briefly thought about asking for protective clothing but gave up on the idea as soon as the manager stepped in and thanked GamePro for the donation of this fine weapon, saying how the Royal Oak was a place that appreciated quality, speaking of a long and dignified tradition of service, and insisting I would be perfectly safe if I kept on my bellhop uniform during the mission. After all, the congressman was wearing nothing but a button-down, a bolo tie, a pair of old jeans and calfskin boots, so why should I expect preferential treatment? Taking the cue, I pushed my bellhop's cap to the preferred rakish angle before shaking hands with the manager on camera to seal our contract.

A few media outlets were allowed to stay in the lobby to document the operation, but for obvious safety and insurance reasons, no cameras could accompany us into the room. A yell of "Grizzly down; all clear!" would be the signal that we'd achieved our objective.

The congressman, cowboy-legged, led the approach. I flanked him on the left, and the hotel manager followed to shut the doors behind us. At the threshold, the congressman paused, unholstered his Colt, and gave a little wave and a yip to the cameras. There was some applause.

As soon as we stepped into the banquet room, though, everything got quiet. The scent of the bear was everywhere—smells of piss and shit and fur and woods, of a creature that had no business being within the walls of the hotel, within any walls. The congressman had dropped back so that we were shoulder to shoulder, and I could smell the fear coming off him too—the eggy stink leaching out under his cologne. He was walking in a crouch and holding his gun at a downward angle, as though he'd forgotten it was there, what it was for. If I'd barked at him then, I believe he would have shat himself. Instead, I asked in a low voice if he'd spotted the target.

He looked around blindly, so I pointed to the far corner of the room, to the nook behind the stage drapes, where the bear sat, squat and huge amid the stacks of red plush chairs, pawing at a lectern it had knocked over. Its fur was bristled and greying around the neck, its eyes beady and black. In its size and strength and capacity for damage, it was a monster. But as the congressman remembered the pistol in his hands and raised it to take aim, the thing just looked dumbly back, as though it were embarrassed to find itself in such a stupid predicament, as though it simply wanted fish and couldn't imagine why none were available, or how the river from which it drew its meat had disappeared. From where we stood, the shot was too long, and the congressman knew it. He looked back at me, expectant, and I gestured to stay low and move in toward the bear, to take cover behind the tables left scattered around the room. He nodded, cocked the hammer of his gun, put a grim look on his face.

"Let's show this motherfucker who's boss," he said, though he was already stammering.

He grunted as he crept forward. I stayed behind him, shotgun ready, wondering how deep the bear's lethargy went, how fast it could spring to life and barrel across the room and break both of our necks with a swipe of its mitt. It stayed put, though, prying splinters from the lectern, shaking its head. We crept from table to table to take up a shielded position around twenty paces from the bear; it didn't so much as snuffle at us. Only when the congressman rose and straightened his back and held out his Colt with both hands—and just stood there, shaking, while the seconds ticked past—did it finally look over, raise a paw to swat at the lectern, and disgorge a stupefied roar.

When the congressman's knees buckled, I knew. He collapsed back behind the table, his whole body quaking. He looked at me and the fear was like jaundice on his face: yellow, inflamed.

"I can't," he said. "I can't."

"Have you ever shot anything before, sir?"

"We're not looking at a fucking duck, are we? Goddamnit, son!"

Whatever he summoned then to convince himself of the best path forward must be that quality all men of power possess, which allows them to focus without distraction on the absolute present, their certainty distilled so its purity can't be questioned when others are asked to drink of its cup. That, or it was just the potency of his fear—the same bone-shaking terror I'd known so intimately that this faceoff with a cornered grizzly played like an exercise, a routine chore.

"Look, I'm sure we all understand our roles here tonight," the congressman said and held out the Colt. I shook my head and gestured at the shotgun, but the congressman waggled the Colt at me and said, "No. It can't go down like that." I took the heavy old piece from him—the one the congressman was known to say he wouldn't even let his wife touch—and stood to take a bead on the grizzly.

I wanted so much for it to stand up. I wished for it, *willed* it, to get indignant and extend to its full height, flash its teeth and pound its chest and charge me at full run. I took a few steps toward it, sights lined up at its glassy black eye. The damn thing didn't move. The absence of its fellow creatures had cloaked its senses like a burlap cowl; it had become lost among the ghosts of its dead brothers and sisters, fumbling through phantom woods no more improbable to it than the real ones it had been torn from, and knew it would never again see. The grizzly knew it was alone, and that the creatures who'd brought it here did not wish it well. I would say that's what allowed me to do it, finally: the anger I felt that, after its first burst of terrified rage, this fearsome thing had become so useless, so neutered and disoriented by the environment of the hotel that it stopped knowing how to defend itself. I would say that, except I would have killed it anyway. As it happened, it just took a little less effort.

In fact, I had no trouble at all walking ten paces and planting two quick shots into its face, one into each eye, the expansion bullets taking the whole crown off the head and throwing fur-flecked bone and pink splatter all over the velvet stage curtains. Once the bear had slumped over in its mess, I put another round into its heart, to stop it from twitching. I knew the animal was dead—knew sure enough what dead looked like—but for good measure I leaned over and held my hand in front of its nose to make sure the breath was gone. The smell of sulphur and burnt metal and gamey blood filled my nose, and I thought for a countless time how it was all the same— bears or warriors or children—all just a pulpy tangle of pink meat and brittle bone under a thinness of pleading skin.

Turning from the bear, I saw the congressman standing where I'd left him, hands clutching the lip of the upturned table, looking at me with something like hatred. The ruddy cast had returned to his jaw, his chin had stopped trembling, and righteousness was gathering in his eyes like a thunder-cloud. He couldn't stand it—the ways in which he needed me, and did not. He couldn't tolerate how expendable I was, how useful and anonymous and effective. There was still fear in his look too, and I knew that while he hated me, he was also afraid of me, as many others had been, and had been right to be.

We faced each other for a few seconds. I had both guns, and the blood of a dead bear on my uniform. The congressman had nothing on his person but a sweat-thinned Egyptian cotton shirt. Yet he implied, in simply being there in that room, the huge apparatus he carried on his back, the political connections and money, the reputation, the potency of his belief. I didn't even make him ask—what good would it have done? I couldn't imagine my situation being better than it was. My sister had pulled a lot of strings to get me the job, a second chance as a bellhop with the city's best hotel. That was as good as it got for men like me.

I walked over to the congressman and handed him the Colt. "Two in the eyes, and one in the heart," I said. He took the gun and nodded and gestured for me to take my place behind him on the left. I did so without comment.

"Grizzly down!" he shouted, the confidence returned to his voice, the zeal of the preacher. "All clear!"

The famous photo from that day shows the congressman and the hotel manager in Banquet Room C shaking hands in front of the bloody carcass, well pleased at how they'd managed to avert the crisis, save the dignity of an historic landmark, and prove what you could accomplish when all the waffling stopped and you just let people do what they did best, be it a question of varmints or pipelines. I knew enough to stand back as the flashbulbs began popping, the two men stepping up to field questions while I hugged the shadows, trying to fade invisible against the backdrop.

Likewise, you'll find no credit underneath the grizzly's head, which is still hanging in the hotel lobby, mounted over the main staircase, ruined skull and all. There's not even a mention of my role—and of that I'm not sorry. It only became clear later on that it was one of the last bears, and I'd want no curse nor accolade I might receive if my part in finishing off that once-feared species were more widely known. It's enough that now when I speak of my past, I can tell this story of how the grizzly came to hang here, a testament to the sad appetites of powerful men, and not of that other past, the one I spent so long trying to lose.

ABOUT THE CONTRIBUTORS

Carleigh Baker is a Métis/Icelandic writer. Her work has appeared in *subTerrain, PRISM International, Joyland*, and *This Magazine*. She won the Lush Triumphant Literary Award for short fiction in 2012, and has been nominated for a National Magazine Award. Her first book, a collection of short stories titled *Bad Endings*, is forthcoming with Anvil Press in spring 2017. She is the current editor of *Joyland* Vancouver.

Charlie Fiset is a gold-miner's daughter from northern Ontario who has recently completed an M.A. in Creative Writing at the University of New Brunswick. Her first print publication, "Maggie's Farm," was included in *The Journey Prize Stories* 27. "If I Ever See the Sun" is her second publication. She is currently at work on a novel and a short story collection.

Mahak Jain's writings have appeared in *Humber Literary Review, Joyland Magazine, The New Quarterly*, and *Room Magazine*. She has placed second in *Humber Literary Review*'s Emerging Writers Fiction Contest and been longlisted for *PRISM international*'s Short Fiction Contest. Her first book for children, *Maya*, was released in spring 2016. She holds an M.F.A. in Creative Writing from the University of Guelph, where she completed a short story collection, including the story "The Origin of Jaanvi." She was born in Delhi and has also lived in Dubai, Massachusetts, New Jersey, and Montreal. She currently resides in Toronto, where she is at work on a novel.

Colette Langlois was raised in the Northwest Territories, and has lived most of her life there when not otherwise wandering the blue-green planet. "The Emigrants," imagined on the Isle of Iona, written in the Colorado Rockies, and edited in the Algarve, was her first fiction publication. She currently resides in Edmonton, where she is working on a short story collection, a novella, a novel, and a Masters of Science.

Alex Leslie has published a collection of short stories, *People Who Disappear* (Freehand, 2012), shortlisted for a Lambda Award for debut fiction, and a collection of prose poems, *The things I heard about you* (Nightwood, 2014), shortlisted for the Robert Kroetsch Award for Innovative Poetry. Alex was the recipient of the 2015 Dayne Ogilvie Prize from the Writers' Trust of Canada. "The Person You Want to See" is part of a collection of short stories in progress entitled *We All Need to Eat*. Alex is also currently at work on a collection of prose poems and microfictions entitled *Vancouver for Beginners*.

Andrew MacDonald lives in Toronto and New England, where he's finishing a novel. "Progress on a Genetic Level" is the fourth story of his to be included in *The Journey Prize Stories*.

J.R. McConvey is a writer from Toronto. His short fiction has appeared in *The Malahat Review*, *EVENT*, *Joyland*, *The Dalhousie Review*, *The Puritan*, and other publications, and has been shortlisted for the Matrix Lit POP award and the Bristol Short Story Prize. His story, "The Last Ham," is available as an e-book single from House of Anansi Digital. He is also a documentary producer whose work includes the award-winning *National Parks Project*, and an occasional poet and journalist. He recently finished his first novel.

Paige Cooper's work has appeared in *The Fiddlehead, Gulf Coast Online, Michigan Quarterly Review, Cosmonauts Avenue,* and *Matrix.* Stories are forthcoming in *Minola Review, Carousel,* and *Best Canadian Stories 2016.* Biblioasis will put out her first book, *Zolitūde,* in 2017. She lives in Montreal.

Souvankham Thammavongsa is the author of three poetry books, the most recent of which, *Light,* won the Trillium Book Award for Poetry. Her story "How to Pronounce Knife" was shortlisted for the 2015 Commonwealth Short Story Prize, and other stories have appeared in *NOON, The Puritan, Ricepaper,* and other places. She has been in residence at Yaddo. Currently, Thammavongsa is completing a collection of short stories and a memoir of her childhood.

For more information about the publications that submitted to this year's competition, The Journey Prize, and *The Journey Prize Stories*, please visit www.facebook.com/TheJourneyPrize.

EVENT features the very best in contemporary writing from Canada and abroad, from literary heavyweights to up-and-comers. For over four decades, *EVENT* has consistently published award-winning fiction, poetry, non-fiction, notes on writing, and critical reviews—all topped off by stunning Canadian cover art. Stories first published in *EVENT* regularly appear in the *Best Canadian Stories* and *Journey Prize Stories* anthologies, and recently won both the Gold and Silver National Magazine Awards in Fiction in (2012 and 2011), and Western Magazine Awards in Fiction in (2012 and 2010). *EVENT* is also home to Canada's longest-running annual non-fiction contest and its Reading Service for Writers. Editor: Shasi Bhat. Managing Editor: Ian Cockfield. Fiction Editor: Christine Dewar. Submissions and correspondence: *EVENT*, P.O. Box 2503, New Westminster, British Columbia, V3L 5B2. Email (queries only): event@douglascollege.ca Website: www.eventmagazine.ca

The Fiddlehead, Atlantic Canada's longest-running literary journal, publishes poetry, short fiction, book reviews, and creative non-fiction. It appears four times a year, sponsors a contest for fiction and for poetry that awards a total of $5,000 in prizes, including the $2,000 Ralph Gustafson Poetry Prize and the $2,000 short fiction prize. *The Fiddlehead* welcomes all good writing in English, from anywhere, looking always for that element of freshness and surprise. Editor: Ross Leckie. Submissions and correspondence: *The Fiddlehead*, Campus House, 11 Garland Court, University of New Brunswick, P.O. Box 4400, Fredericton, New Brunswick, E3B 5A3. E-mail (queries only): fiddlehd@unb.ca Website: www.TheFiddlehead. ca Twitter: @TheFiddlehd You can also find *The Fiddlehead* on Facebook.

Based on the idea that fiction is an international movement supported by local communities, **Joyland** is a literary magazine that selects stories regionally. Our editors work with authors connected to locales across North America, including New York, Los Angeles, Vancouver, and Toronto, as well as places underrepresented in cultural media. New content appears weekly and we go into print twice yearly with *Retro*. Publishers: Brian Joseph Davis, Emily Schultz. Managing Editor: Kyle Lucia Wu. Senior Editors: Eleanor Kriseman (New York), Kara Levy (San Francisco), Lisa Locascio (Los Angeles), David McGimpsey (Montreal and Atlantic Canada), Kathryn Mockler (Toronto and Vancouver), Anna Prushinskaya (Midwest), Charles McLeod (Pacific Northwest). No hardcopy submissions accepted. Please see Joylandmagazine.com for submission details or contact joylandsubmissions@gmail.com.

The Malahat Review is a quarterly journal of contemporary poetry, fiction, and creative non-fiction by both new and celebrated writers. Summer issues feature the winners of *Malahat*'s Novella and Long Poem prizes, held in alternate years; the fall issues feature the winners of the Far Horizons Award for emerging writers, alternating between poetry and fiction each year; the winter issues feature the winners of the Constance Rooke Creative Non-fiction Prize; and the spring issues feature winners of the Open Season Awards in all three genres (poetry, fiction, and creative non-fiction). All issues feature covers by noted Canadian visual artists and include reviews of Canadian books. Editor: John Barton. Assistant Editor: Rhonda Batchelor. Submissions and correspondence: *The Malahat Review*, University of Victoria, P.O. Box 1700, Station CSC, Victoria, British Columbia, V8W 2Y2. E-mail: malahat@uvic.ca Website: www.malahatreview.ca Twitter: @malahatreview

PRISM international, the oldest literary magazine in Western Canada, was established in 1959 by Earle Birney at the University of British Columbia. Published four times a year, *PRISM* features short fiction, poetry, creative non-fiction, drama, and translations. *PRISM* editors select work based on originality and quality, and the magazine showcases work from both new and established writers from Canada and around the world. *PRISM* holds three exemplary annual competitions for short fiction, literary non-fiction, and poetry, and awards the Earle Birney Prize for Poetry to an outstanding poet whose work was featured in *PRISM* in the preceding year. Executive Editors: Jennifer Lori and Claire Matthews. Prose Editor: Christopher Evans. Poetry Editor: Dominique Bernier-Cormier. Reviews Editor: Anita Bedell. Submissions and correspondence: *PRISM international*, Creative Writing Program, The University of British Columbia, Buchanan

E-462, 1866 Main Mall, Vancouver, British Columbia, V6T 1Z1. Website:www.prismmagazine.ca

Since its foundation in 2006, **The Puritan** has published work by, and interviews with, some of Canada's finest literary talents. It is one of very few online literary magazines that offers substantial honorariums for its contributors. In 2012, *The Puritan* was one of the first two online magazines to have its fiction featured in the *Journey Prize Stories*. The magazine routinely features guest editors for its regular issues and judges for its annual literary contest, The Thomas Morton Memorial Prize, which now awards over $4,000 in prizes. Past guest editors and contest judges have included Katherena Vermette, Kathryn Kuitenbrouwer, Sonnet L'Abbé, Rawi Hage, Miriam Toews, Zsuzsi Gartner, and Margaret Atwood. *The Puritan* also runs *The Town Crier*, one of the best—and most productive—literary blogs in the country. Senior Editors: Spencer Gordon and Tyler Willis. Website: www.puritan-magazine.com Submissions: www.puritan-magazine.com/submissions Blog: www.town-crier.ca.

Beginning as a modest eight-page newsletter for the Asian Canadian Writers' Workshop (ACWW), **Ricepaper** has evolved into a magazine distributed coast-to-coast, publishing the new voices coming out of the Asian Canadian arts and literary community. Since 1994, *Ricepaper* has showcased Asian Canadian literature, culture, and the arts, and it continues to be the only Canadian literary magazine of its kind with an Asian Canadian perspective, publishing new poetry, fiction, drama, graphic novel, translation, and almost every other kind of creative writing from writers across the country, as well as cultural reviews of books, theatre, and film. The body of work coming out of the Asian Canadian artists and writers' community is prolific and growing. *Ricepaper* profiles and interviews the leading and up-and-coming artists and writers in this community. Executive Editor: Allan Cho. Fiction Editor: Karla Comanda. Submissions and correspondence: *Ricepaper* magazine, PO Box 74174, Hillcrest RPO, Vancouver, BC, V5V 5L8. Email: info@ricepapermagazine.ca Website: www.ricepapermagazine.ca

The Rusty Toque is a contemporary online literary and arts journal. We strive to publish innovative literary writing, film, comics, reviews, and visual art from new and established writers and artists in the spring and fall of each year. We also have an ongoing interview series, a review series, and a special features section. We are supported through a grant from The Canada Council for the Arts. Publisher: Kathryn Mockler, Senior Editors: David Poolman, Aaron Schneider, Jacqueline Valencia. Email: therustytoque@gmail.com Website: www. therustytoque.com

SubTerrain Magazine's mandate is to publish contemporary and sometimes controversial Canadian fiction, poetry, non-fiction, and visual art. Presented in an attractive and accessible magazine format, *subTerrain* features interviews, timely commentary, and book reviews in every issue. Ninety percent of the magazine's editorial content is original and previously unpublished material from new writers and artists. *subTerrain* is praised by both writers and readers for featuring work that might not find a home in more conservative periodicals. The magazine is home to the Lush Triumphant Literary Awards, awarding $3,000 in prizes each year, plus publication. *subTerrain* itself has been recognized by numerous awards over the years, including the National Magazine Awards, Western Magazine Awards and others. *subTerrain*'s main objective in fulfilling its mandate is to continually challenge the status quo—by showcasing the best in progressive writing and ideas, *subTerrain* seeks to expand the definition of Canadian literary and artistic culture. Editor-in-Chief: Brian Kaufman. Managing Editor: Natasha Sanders-Kay. Submissions and correspondence: *subTerrain Magazine*, P.O. Box 3008 MPO, Vancouver, BC, V6B 3X5. Submissions info, subscriptions, and samples at www.subterrain.ca

Taddle Creek often is asked to define itself and, just as often, it tends to refuse to do so. But it will say this: each issue of the magazine contains a multitude of things between its snazzily illustrated covers, including, but not limited to, fiction, poetry, comics, art, interviews, and feature stories. It's an odd mix, to be sure, which is why *Taddle Creek* refers to itself somewhat oddly as a "general-interest literary magazine." Work presented in *Taddle Creek* is humorous, poignant, ephemeral, urban, and rarely overly earnest, though not usually all at once. *Taddle Creek* takes its mission to be the journal for those who detest everything the literary magazine has become in the twenty-first century very seriously. Editor-in-Chief: Conan Tobias. Correspondence: *Taddle Creek*, P.O. Box 611, Stn. P, Toronto, Ontario M5S 2Y4. E-mail: editor@taddlecreekmag. com. Website: taddlecreekmag.com.

Submissions were also received from the following publications:

Agnes and True
www.agnesandtrue.com

The Antigonish Review
(Antigonish, NS)
www.antigonishreview.com

Cosmonauts Avenue
(Montreal, QC)
www.cosmonautsavenue.com

The Dalhousie Review
(Halifax, NS)
www.dalhousiereview.dal.ca

The Danforth Review
(Toronto, ON)
www.danforthreview.com

FreeFall Magazine
(Calgary, AB)
www.freefallmagazine.ca

Glass Buffalo
(Edmonton, AB)
www.glassbuffalo.com

Grain Magazine
(Regina, SK)
www.grainmagazine.ca

The Humber Literary Review
(Toronto, ON)
www.humberliterary
review.com

The Impressment Gang
(Halifax, NS)
www.theimpressment
gang.com

Little Fiction / Big Truths
(Toronto, ON)
www.littlefiction.com

Matrix Magazine
(Montreal QC)
www.matrixmagazine.org

Newfoundland Quarterly
(St. John's, NL)
www.mun.ca/nq

The New Orphic Review
(Nelson, BC)

The New Quarterly
(Waterloo, ON)
www.tnq.ca

(parenthetical)
(Toronto, ON)
www.wordsonpagespress.
com/parenthetical

Plenitude Magazine
www.plenitudemagazine.ca

Prairie Fire
(Winnipeg, MB)
www.prairiefire.ca

*The Prairie Journal of
Canadian Literature*
(Calgary, AB)
www.prairiejournal.org

PULP Literature
(Vancouver, BC)
www.pulpliterature.com

Riddle Fence
(St. John's NL)
www.riddlefence.com

Room Magazine
(Vancouver, BC)
www.roommagazine.com

This Magazine
(Toronto, ON)
www.this.org

The Walrus
(Toronto, ON)
www.thewalrus.ca

PREVIOUS CONTRIBUTING AUTHORS

* Winners of the $10,000 Journey Prize
** Co-winners of the $10,000 Journey Prize

1

1989

SELECTED WITH ALISTAIR MACLEOD

Ven Begamudré, "Word Games"
David Bergen, "Where You're From"
Lois Braun, "The Pumpkin-Eaters"
Constance Buchanan, "Man with Flying Genitals"
Ann Copeland, "Obedience"
Marion Douglas, "Flags"
Frances Itani, "An Evening in the Café"
Diane Keating, "The Crying Out"
Thomas King, "One Good Story, That One"
Holley Rubinsky, "Rapid Transits"*
Jean Rysstad, "Winter Baby"
Kevin Van Tighem, "Whoopers"
M.G. Vassanji, "In the Quiet of a Sunday Afternoon"
Bronwen Wallace, "Chicken 'N' Ribs"
Armin Wiebe, "Mouse Lake"
Budge Wilson, "Waiting"

2

1990

SELECTED WITH LEON ROOKE; GUY VANDERHAEGHE

André Alexis, "Despair: Five Stories of Ottawa"
Glen Allen, "The Hua Guofeng Memorial Warehouse"
Marusia Bociurkiw, "Mama, Donya"
Virgil Burnett, "Billfrith the Dreamer"
Margaret Dyment, "Sacred Trust"
Cynthia Flood, "My Father Took a Cake to France"*
Douglas Glover, "Story Carved in Stone"
Terry Griggs, "Man with the Axe"
Rick Hillis, "Limbo River"

Thomas King, "The Dog I Wish I Had, I Would Call It Helen"
K.D. Miller, "Sunrise Till Dark"
Jennifer Mitton, "Let Them Say"
Lawrence O'Toole, "Goin' to Town with Katie Ann"
Kenneth Radu, "A Change of Heart"
Jenifer Sutherland, "Table Talk"
Wayne Tefs, "Red Rock and After"

3
1991
SELECTED WITH JANE URQUHART

Donald Aker, "The Invitation"
Anton Baer, "Yukon"
Allan Barr, "A Visit from Lloyd"
David Bergen, "The Fall"
Rai Berzins, "Common Sense"
Diana Hartog, "Theories of Grief"
Diane Keating, "The Salem Letters"
Yann Martel, "The Facts Behind the Helsinki Roccamatios"*
Jennifer Mitton, "Polaroid"
Sheldon Oberman, "This Business with Elijah"
Lynn Podgurny, "Till Tomorrow, Maple Leaf Mills"
James Riseborough, "She Is Not His Mother"
Patricia Stone, "Living on the Lake"

4
1992
SELECTED WITH SANDRA BIRDSELL

David Bergen, "The Bottom of the Glass"
Maria A. Billion, "No Miracles Sweet Jesus"
Judith Cowan, "By the Big River"
Steven Heighton, "How Beautiful upon the Mountains"
Steven Heighton, "A Man Away from Home Has No Neighbours"
L. Rex Kay, "Travelling"
Rozena Maart, "No Rosa, No District Six"*
Guy Malet De Carteret, "Rainy Day"
Carmelita McGrath, "Silence"
Michael Mirolla, "A Theory of Discontinuous Existence"
Diane Juttner Perreault, "Bella's Story"
Eden Robinson, "Traplines"

5
1993
SELECTED WITH GUY VANDERHAEGHE

Caroline Adderson, "Oil and Dread"

David Bergen, "La Rue Prevette"

Marina Endicott, "With the Band"

Dayv James-French, "Cervine"

Michael Kenyon, "Durable Tumblers"

K.D. Miller, "A Litany in Time of Plague"

Robert Mullen, "Flotsam"

Gayla Reid, "Sister Doyle's Men"*

Oakland Ross, "Bang-bang"

Robert Sherrin, "Technical Battle for Trial Machine"

Carol Windley, "The Etruscans"

6
1994
SELECTED WITH DOUGLAS GLOVER;
JUDITH CHANT (CHAPTERS)

Anne Carson, "Water Margins: An Essay on Swimming by My Brother"

Richard Cumyn, "The Sound He Made"

Genni Gunn, "Versions"

Melissa Hardy, "Long Man the River"*

Robert Mullen, "Anomie"

Vivian Payne, "Free Falls"

Jim Reil, "Dry"

Robyn Sarah, "Accept My Story"

Joan Skogan, "Landfall"

Dorothy Speak, "Relatives in Florida"

Alison Wearing, "Notes from Under Water"

7
1995
SELECTED WITH M.G. VASSANJI;
RICHARD BACHMANN (A DIFFERENT DRUMMER BOOKS)

Michelle Alfano, "Opera"

Mary Borsky, "Maps of the Known World"

Gabriella Goliger, "Song of Ascent"

Elizabeth Hay, "Hand Games"

Shaena Lambert, "The Falling Woman"

Elise Levine, "Boy"

Roger Burford Mason, "The Rat-Catcher's Kiss"
Antanas Sileika, "Going Native"
Kathryn Woodward, "Of Marranos and Gilded Angels"*

8
1996
SELECTED WITH OLIVE SENIOR;
BEN McNALLY (NICHOLAS HOARE LTD.)
Rick Bowers, "Dental Bytes"
David Elias, "How I Crossed Over"
Elyse Gasco, "Can You Wave Bye Bye, Baby?"*
Danuta Gleed, "Bones"
Elizabeth Hay, "The Friend"
Linda Holeman, "Turning the Worm"
Elaine Littman, "The Winner's Circle"
Murray Logan, "Steam"
Rick Maddocks, "Lessons from the Sputnik Diner"
K.D. Miller, "Egypt Land"
Gregor Robinson, "Monster Gaps"
Alma Subasic, "Dust"

9
1997
SELECTED WITH NINO RICCI; NICHOLAS PASHLEY
(UNIVERSITY OF TORONTO BOOKSTORE)
Brian Bartlett, "Thomas, Naked"
Dennis Bock, "Olympia"
Kristen den Hartog, "Wave"
Gabriella Goliger, "Maladies of the Inner Ear"**
Terry Griggs, "Momma Had a Baby"
Mark Anthony Jarman, "Righteous Speedboat"
Judith Kalman, "Not for Me a Crown of Thorns"
Andrew Mullins, "The World of Science"
Sasenarine Persaud, "Canada Geese and Apple Chatney"
Anne Simpson, "Dreaming Snow"**
Sarah Withrow, "Ollie"
Terence Young, "The Berlin Wall"

10

1998

SELECTED BY PETER BUITENHUIS; HOLLEY RUBINSKY; CELIA DUTHIE (DUTHIE BOOKS LTD.)

John Brooke, "The Finer Points of Apples"*

Ian Colford, "The Reason for the Dream"

Libby Creelman, "Cruelty"

Michael Crummey, "Serendipity"

Stephen Guppy, "Downwind"

Jane Eaton Hamilton, "Graduation"

Elise Levine, "You Are You Because Your Little Dog Loves You"

Jean McNeil, "Bethlehem"

Liz Moore, "Eight-Day Clock"

Edward O'Connor, "The Beatrice of Victoria College"

Tim Rogers, "Scars and Other Presents"

Denise Ryan, "Marginals, Vivisections, and Dreams"

Madeleine Thien, "Simple Recipes"

Cheryl Tibbetts, "Flowers of Africville"

11

1999

SELECTED BY LESLEY CHOYCE; SHELDON CURRIE; MARY-JO ANDERSON (FROG HOLLOW BOOKS)

Mike Barnes, "In Florida"

Libby Creelman, "Sunken Island"

Mike Finigan, "Passion Sunday"

Jane Eaton Hamilton, "Territory"

Mark Anthony Jarman, "Travels into Several Remote Nations of the World"

Barbara Lambert, "Where the Bodies Are Kept"

Linda Little, "The Still"

Larry Lynch, "The Sitter"

Sandra Sabatini, "The One With the News"

Sharon Steams, "Brothers"

Mary Walters, "Show Jumping"

Alissa York, "The Back of the Bear's Mouth"*

12
2000

**SELECTED BY CATHERINE BUSH; HAL NIEDZVIECKI;
MARC GLASSMAN (PAGES BOOKS AND MAGAZINES)**

Andrew Gray, "The Heart of the Land"
Lee Henderson, "Sheep Dub"
Jessica Johnson, "We Move Slowly"
John Lavery, "The Premier's New Pyjamas"
J.A. McCormack, "Hearsay"
Nancy Richler, "Your Mouth Is Lovely"
Andrew Smith, "Sightseeing"
Karen Solie, "Onion Calendar"
Timothy Taylor, "Doves of Townsend"*
Timothy Taylor, "Pope's Own"
Timothy Taylor, "Silent Cruise"
R.M. Vaughan, "Swan Street"

13
2001

**SELECTED BY ELYSE GASCO; MICHAEL HELM;
MICHAEL NICHOLSON (INDIGO BOOKS & MUSIC INC.)**

Kevin Armstrong, "The Cane Field"*
Mike Barnes, "Karaoke Mon Amour"
Heather Birrell, "Machaya"
Heather Birrell, "The Present Perfect"
Craig Boyko, "The Gun"
Vivette J. Kady, "Anything That Wiggles"
Billie Livingston, "You're Taking All the Fun Out of It"
Annabel Lyon, "Fishes"
Lisa Moore, "The Way the Light Is"
Heather O'Neill, "Little Suitcase"
Susan Rendell, "In the Chambers of the Sea"
Tim Rogers, "Watch"
Margrith Schraner, "Dream Dig"

14
2002
SELECTED BY ANDRÉ ALEXIS;
DEREK McCORMACK; DIANE SCHOEMPERLEN

Mike Barnes, "Cogagwee"

Geoffrey Brown, "Listen"

Jocelyn Brown, "Miss Canada"*

Emma Donoghue, "What Remains"

Jonathan Goldstein, "You Are a Spaceman With Your Head Under the Bathroom Stall Door"

Robert McGill, "Confidence Men"

Robert McGill, "The Stars Are Falling"

Nick Melling, "Philemon"

Robert Mullen, "Alex the God"

Karen Munro, "The Pool"

Leah Postman, "Being Famous"

Neil Smith, "Green Fluorescent Protein"

15
2003
SELECTED BY MICHELLE BERRY;
TIMOTHY TAYLOR; MICHAEL WINTER

Rosaria Campbell, "Reaching"

Hilary Dean, "The Lemon Stories"

Dawn Rae Downton, "Hansel and Gretel"

Anne Fleming, "Gay Dwarves of America"

Elyse Friedman, "Truth"

Charlotte Gill, "Hush"

Jessica Grant, "My Husband's Jump"*

Jacqueline Honnet, "Conversion Classes"

S.K. Johannesen, "Resurrection"

Avner Mandelman, "Cuckoo"

Tim Mitchell, "Night Finds Us"

Heather O'Neill, "The Difference Between Me and Goldstein"

16
2004
SELECTED BY ELIZABETH HAY; LISA MOORE; MICHAEL REDHILL

Anar Ali, "Baby Khaki's Wings"

Kenneth Bonert, "Packers and Movers"

Jennifer Clouter, "Benny and the Jets"

Daniel Griffin, "Mercedes Buyer's Guide"
Michael Kissinger, "Invest in the North"
Devin Krukoff, "The Last Spark"*
Elaine McCluskey, "The Watermelon Social"
William Metcalfe, "Nice Big Car, Rap Music Coming Out the Window"
Lesley Millard, "The Uses of the Neckerchief"
Adam Lewis Schroeder, "Burning the Cattle at Both Ends"
Michael V. Smith, "What We Wanted"
Neil Smith, "Isolettes"
Patricia Rose Young, "Up the Clyde on a Bike"

17
2005
SELECTED BY JAMES GRAINGER AND NANCY LEE

Randy Boyagoda, "Rice and Curry Yacht Club"
Krista Bridge, "A Matter of Firsts"
Josh Byer, "Rats, Homosex, Saunas, and Simon"
Craig Davidson, "Failure to Thrive"
McKinley M. Hellenes, "Brighter Thread"
Catherine Kidd, "Green-Eyed Beans"
Pasha Malla, "The Past Composed"
Edward O'Connor, "Heard Melodies Are Sweet"
Barbara Romanik, "Seven Ways into Chandigarh"
Sandra Sabatini, "The Dolphins at Sainte Marie"
Matt Shaw, "Matchbook for a Mother's Hair"*
Richard Simas, "Anthropologies"
Neil Smith, "Scrapbook"
Emily White, "Various Metals"

18
2006
SELECTED BY STEVEN GALLOWAY;
ZSUZSI GARTNER; ANNABEL LYON

Heather Birrell, "BriannaSusannaAlana"*
Craig Boyko, "The Baby"
Craig Boyko, "The Beloved Departed"
Nadia Bozak, "Heavy Metal Housekeeping"
Lee Henderson, "Conjugation"
Melanie Little, "Wrestling"
Matthew Rader, "The Lonesome Death of Joseph Fey"
Scott Randall, "Law School"

Sarah Selecky, "Throwing Cotton"
Damian Tarnopolsky, "Sleepy"
Martin West, "Cretacea"
David Whitton, "The Eclipse"
Clea Young, "Split"

19
2007
SELECTED BY CAROLINE ADDERSON;
DAVID BEZMOZGIS; DIONNE BRAND
Andrew J. Borkowski, "Twelve Versions of Lech"
Craig Boyko, "OZY"*
Grant Buday, "The Curve of the Earth"
Nicole Dixon, "High-Water Mark"
Krista Foss, "Swimming in Zanzibar"
Pasha Malla, "Respite"
Alice Petersen, "After Summer"
Patricia Robertson, "My Hungarian Sister"
Rebecca Rosenblum, "Chilly Girl"
Nicholas Ruddock, "How Eunice Got Her Baby"
Jean Van Loon, "Stardust"

20
2008
SELECTED BY LYNN COADY; HEATHER O'NEILL; NEIL SMITH
Théodora Armstrong, "Whale Stories"
Mike Christie, "Goodbye Porkpie Hat"
Anna Leventhal, "The Polar Bear at the Museum"
Naomi K. Lewis, "The Guiding Light"
Oscar Martens, "Breaking on the Wheel"
Dana Mills, "Steaming for Godthab"
Saleema Nawaz, "My Three Girls"*
Scott Randall, "The Gifted Class"
S. Kennedy Sobol, "Some Light Down"
Sarah Steinberg, "At Last at Sea"
Clea Young, "Chaperone"

21
2009
SELECTED BY CAMILLA GIBB;
LEE HENDERSON; REBECCA ROSENBLUM

Daniel Griffin, "The Last Great Works of Alvin Cale"
Jesus Hardwell, "Easy Living"
Paul Headrick, "Highlife"
Sarah Keevil, "Pyro"
Adrian Michael Kelly, "Lure"
Fran Kimmel, "Picturing God's Ocean"
Lynne Kutsukake, "Away"
Alexander MacLeod, "Miracle Mile"
Dave Margoshes, "The Wisdom of Solomon"
Shawn Syms, "On the Line"
Sarah L. Taggart, "Deaf"
Yasuko Thanh, "Floating Like the Dead"*

22
2010
SELECTED BY PASHA MALLA; JOAN THOMAS; ALISSA YORK

Carolyn Black, "Serial Love"
Andrew Boden, "Confluence of Spoors"
Laura Boudreau, "The Dead Dad Game"
Devon Code, "Uncle Oscar"*
Danielle Egan, "Publicity"
Krista Foss, "The Longitude of Okay"
Lynne Kutsukake, "Mating"
Ben Lof, "When in the Field with Her at His Back"
Andrew MacDonald, "Eat Fist!"
Eliza Robertson, "Ship's Log"
Mike Spry, "Five Pounds Short and Apologies to Nelson Algren"
Damian Tarnopolsky, "Laud We the Gods"

23
2011
SELECTED BY ALEXANDER MacLEOD;
ALISON PICK; SARAH SELECKY

Jay Brown, "The Girl from the War"
Michael Christie, "The Extra"
Seyward Goodhand, "The Fur Trader's Daughter"
Miranda Hill, "Petitions to Saint Chronic"*

Fran Kimmel, "Laundry Day"
Ross Klatte, "First-Calf Heifer"
Michelle Serwatuk, "My Eyes Are Dim"
Jessica Westhead, "What I Would Say"
Michelle Winters, "Toupée"
D.W. Wilson, "The Dead Roads"

24
2012
SELECTED BY MICHAEL CHRISTIE;
KATHRYN KUITENBROUWER; KATHLEEN WINTER

Kris Bertin, "Is Alive and Can Move"
Shashi Bhat, "Why I Read *Beowulf*"
Astrid Blodgett, "Ice Break"
Trevor Corkum, "You Were Loved"
Nancy Jo Cullen, "Ashes"
Kevin Hardcastle, "To Have to Wait"
Andrew Hood, "I'm Sorry and Thank You"
Andrew Hood, "Manning"
Grace O'Connell, "The Many Faces of Montgomery Clift"
Jasmina Odor, "Barcelona"
Alex Pugsley, "Crisis on Earth-X"*
Eliza Robertson, "Sea Drift"
Martin West, "My Daughter of the Dead Reeds"

25
2013
SELECTED BY MIRANDA HILL;
MARK MEDLEY; RUSSELL WANGERSKY

Steven Benstead, "Megan's Bus"
Jay Brown, "The Egyptians"
Andrew Forbes, "In the Foothills"
Philip Huynh, "Gulliver's Wife"
Amy Jones, "Team Ninja"
Marnie Lamb, "Mrs. Fujimoto's Wednesday Afternoons"
Doretta Lau, "How Does a Single Blade of Grass Thank the Sun?"
Laura Legge, "It's Raining in Paris"
Natalie Morrill, "Ossicles"
Zoey Leigh Peterson, "Sleep World"
Eliza Robertson, "My Sister Sang"
Naben Ruthnum, "Cinema Rex"*

26
2014
SELECTED BY STEVEN W. BEATTIE; CRAIG DAVIDSON; SALEEMA NAWAZ

Rosaria Campbell, "Probabilities"
Nancy Jo Cullen, "Hashtag Maggie Vandermeer"
M.A. Fox, "Piano Boy"
Kevin Hardcastle, "Old Man Marchuk"
Amy Jones, "Wolves, Cigarettes, Gum"
Tyler Keevil, "Sealskin"*
Jeremy Lanaway, "Downturn"
Andrew MacDonald, "Four Minutes"
Lori McNulty, "Monsoon Season"
Shana Myara, "Remainders"
Julie Roorda, "How to Tell if Your Frog Is Dead"
Leona Theis, "High Beams"
Clea Young, "Juvenile"

27
2015
SELECTED BY ANTONY DE SA, TANIS RIDEOUT, AND CARRIE SNYDER

Charlotte Bondy, "Renaude"
Emily Bossé, "Last Animal Standing on Gentleman's Farm"
Deirdre Dore, "The Wise Baby"*
Charlie Fiset, "Maggie's Farm"
K'ari Fisher, "Mercy Beatrice Wrestles the Noose"
Anna Ling Kaye, "Red Egg and Ginger"
Andrew MacDonald, "The Perfect Man for my Husband"
Madeleine Maillet, "Achille's Death"
Lori McNulty, "Fingernecklace"
Sarah Meehan Sirk, "Moonman"
Ron Schafrick, "Lovely Company"
Georgia Wilder, "Cocoa Divine and the Lightning Police"